more. . .

Also by Sarah Gilbert

DIXIE RIGGS
HAIRDO

Published by
WARNER BOOKS

SARAH GILBERT

SUMMER GLOVES

WARNER BOOKS

A Time Warner Company

WARNER BOOKS EDITION

Cover design by Diane Luger
Cover photograph by Tom Haynes

Warner Books, Inc.
1271 Avenue of the Americas
New York, NY 10020

W A Time Warner Company

Printed in the United States of America

Originally published in hardcover by Warner Books.
First Printed in Paperback: March, 1994

10 9 8 7 6 5 4 3 2 1

With love for Bill, who taught me how to be the kind of daughter a mother could love.
And with love for my mother, who loved me long before Bill came along.

ACKNOWLEDGMENTS

A special thanks to all my friends who were ever daughters and lived to tell the tale: Bennett, Eileen, Elizabeth, Esther, Jamie, Jean, Judith, Kathy, Lynne, Margaret Mahone, Nanscy, Pattygirl, Peg, Roberta, Robin, Virginia, Weezie, Susan, Pam, Harriet, and Zari.

1

God, I've gone and turned into my mother. Even down to the shoes I wear. I can't believe this is me. Standing here looking in the mirror. It's no wonder Flick wants to leave me. When did all this happen? This great transformation from nymph to, well, to this. And why am I just noticing it for the first time? Where have I been?

What really bugs me is this. I've started in on my daughter. Poor unsuspecting thing. There she is, happily being her little old self and I up and whisk her off into beauty queen land. Just like my mother did to me and her mother did to her and undoubtedly her mother would have done to her if there had ever been such a thing back then. And which I vowed I would never do to Evie. But here I am, buying her little beauty queen shoes to match her little beauty queen dress that even Macayla Irvin will not be able to beat. It is the cutest thing you ever saw. It is yellow organdy with white flouncy lace coming out of it in all directions. But that is not the point. The point is, it has these darling little pearls sewn on it to look like happy little doggies chasing their tails around in happy little circles.

See. That's the whole point. My mother would never have let me wear something so original. So neat. She would have had me, did in fact have me, in pink crinoline straight up and down all day long, with no happy doggies to be found. God, I hated those dresses. I used to think, "Damn, if maybe I could just pick out my own dress, I would like being in these stupid contests." After all, they were fun. Some of them were fun. I'd even be willing to say that those were the best days of my life. Not something you'd want your daughter to miss out on.

But I was going to be a little different with my Evie. For instance, I was certainly going to let her have some say in what she wore. So, I let her pick out the dress. Oh sure. At first I balked. No judge would take a dress like that seriously. Then I remembered that time when I lost out to Mary Louise Palance because she was the first girl to wear a poodle skirt for her talent competition.

I can tell you right now. That is the only thing that won that bitch that contest. She certainly couldn't play the piano worth a damn. And me, there I was twirling my baton to beat the band and it was the first, the first, last and only time I did not screw up on that last part where the drums always came in so loud and threw me off. I mean, I'd won many times screwing up, but this was the first time I hadn't dropped it and that bitch Mary Louise goes and takes my prize anyway.

Well, that is neither here nor there. Mary Louise is fat now. She has five kids. She couldn't even fit in any damn bathing suit now, much less win a contest in one. Lord, God, it took me nine months to snap back from having

Evie. I thought I'd never get my stomach back. And those children of Mary Louise's. Talk about a bunch of little fatsos. I would never let my Evie get like that. I keep her on a strict diet, for unfortunately, big thighs run on her daddy's side of the family.

Can you believe that my mother actually mentioned this to me before Flick and I eloped? She told me over and over again that I was going to be sorry for countless numbers of things and that if they didn't bother me, at least those Outlaw thunder thighs should. I remember waving my hand out the window as Flick drove off, going, "Ta-ta, see if I care, Mom," thinking, "Imagine that. You just can't let your entire life go by worrying about your damned thighs. You'd never find happiness."

I also remember thinking that if I did have a little girl who had big fat thighs and was short and, heaven forbid my mother, even wore glasses or something, well hell, she could be a stupid librarian for all I cared. Love would find the way.

Yeah. Right.

Well, I am here to tell you. Love will never find the way. You can let it lead you by the nose and out the door and down the street away from your house and your mother and the only place it's going to lead you is into a mall looking for new clothes and a new hairdo so you won't feel so lousy about yourself all the time.

What do I mean?

Hell, I don't even know anymore. All I know is that Flick has taken off with his coed bitch Audrey, and she doesn't even have half the body I do. And her little face looks like it's been sucked through a tube.

And I stand here, Watermelon Queen 1976, Miss Peach Queen 1977, and believe it or not, Miss South Carolina which led me to be the fourth runner-up at the Miss

America Pageant, which I probably would have won if I hadn't gotten pregnant with Evie. I just couldn't get rid of that little stomach pooch. God, did I protrude in my bathing suit. It looked like I'd been knocking back spaghetti all week and the truth of the matter was, I about starved to death up there in Atlantic City. I was so damned hungry that when I get hungry now, all I can think about is that time when I was standing there in front of Bert Parks with him asking me what I would do to make the world a better place. And me, sucking my stomach in, my lips shaking, stretched over a total beauty queen smile, thinking, "The first thing I'd do is get myself a twenty-seven-inch pizza with everything on it but the kitchen sink, and I'd think about the question while I ate it and then I'd give him my answer."

So. I said, "Well. I'd feed the hungry." Then I went rattling on like some idiot not knowing what I was saying, because what I had planned to talk about was loving thy neighbor and all that Bible spiel that is a surefire winner at any beauty contest. Or was before everyone got so weird and touchy about religion. Damn, I mean, there is just no way to coach your kid on how to answer these questions nowadays because if it is not one thing, it is another. Someone is always dying to jump down your throat about something.

And this is Evie. Last year at the Little Miss Okra Strut, they asked her what she would do to make the world a better place and she stood there for such a long time thinking, that I thought I was going to faint. I'm waving my hands frantically for her to go on, speak up, say something quick, watching Macayla Irvin on the sidelines getting ready to come in for the kill. Finally Evie puts her hand on her chin, a big no-no I just can't break her of, and she says, "I would see to it that everybody got a dog or a cat."

Now I ask you. What the hell was that? Okay, it was cute.

But she wasn't being judged on cute. Hell, if cute was all it took to win a contest, every Tom, Dick or Harry's white trash kid on the block would go up there and compete. But that's not what it takes.

Frankly, I don't know what it takes anymore. If I did, maybe Flick wouldn't be walking out on me now.

Can you imagine? Somewhere I had it in the back of my mind that if I won just enough beauty contests, just the right kind, that I could count on a man to love me and cherish me forever for the rest of my life, amen. And that if I were ever in the malls talking to my girlfriends, listening to them complaining about their stinking cheating husbands, I'd be able to smile to myself and say, "Not me. Not the Watermelon Queen. My marriage is as firm as the Bible." Or something like that. It was a little abstract but it seemed to be a sure thing. I mean, my mother was Miss New Jersey and her husband never screwed out on her. Her second one. I don't know about her first one, my father. He just left.

We weren't exactly the rosy couple to begin with, Flick and me. I can't say it was like in the movies where we dated each other in high school and then got married, maybe broke up once or twice along the way only to get back together again. The truth is, by the time I'd met Flick, I'd slept with just about every judge that ever sat facing me in an evening gown competition. Now this is not as sleazy as it sounds. Well, okay, maybe it is. But when you spend the main part of your life dressing up, there comes a time when you just say, "Screw it," and strip it all off so someone can like you for what you are underneath instead of for what you are all wrapped up in those damned expensive, crisp, pressed clothes. That's all I'm saying. I don't really think it's all that complicated.

In fact, I guess it sounds like I slept my way to the Miss South Carolina Pageant, but that wasn't the case. I knew I'd win on my own. Winning was a cinch. It's just that the only men I ever got to meet were the judges. That was all there was out there for me. If you don't think my mother hawked over me, forget it! She wouldn't let a boy come within fifteen yards. Also, let me say right now in my own defense, I wouldn't stoop so low as to go with one of those lady judges, which is what little Macayla Irvin did once. I think. I wouldn't swear to it, because I am not into slandering, but I would slap my last dollar down on a bet saying she did.

I'll get into that later.

But Flick, he was the first man I ever did it with who didn't have any connections with the beauty queen world. God. What freedom. I'd spent my entire life with eighty thousand men telling me to lose three more inches off my breasts, waist, hips, thighs and then I run up against this one man who says, "Pammy, you are too skinny. Look at you. You look like a stick figure. Let's go feed you somewhere." I fell spiraling down, hopelessly in love. Have been, in fact, up to and including this very day when he walked out of here mad again. He didn't even say where he was going this time.

We don't ever talk enough for that anymore.

I think college screwed Flick up. He was a nice boy until he decided to become an English professor. I didn't even know he liked reading. It didn't even cross my mind. Until one day he said, "Pammy, you never read. Why don't you read?" Then after that, only then did I realize that he had always been reading.

It became this huge issue for him. He started giving me all these newspaper articles about economics and politics and I'm sitting there thinking, "Well, this is all just fine and dandy, Flick. I vote. It's not like I don't vote. But I cannot follow word one of this stuff." Then it became like a bad song he always sang around me. It was worse than one of those tunes you think you will never get out of your head, because eventually you do forget those. But I could never get Flick saying "I just don't understand why you don't read" out of mine.

So what did I do? Well, I did what any loving wife would do. I went to the library and started checking out books. And suddenly I saw. Yes. Reading was fun. I even got to the point where I couldn't put a book down for anything. I'd be all captured up in it, sitting on the edge of the bed and there it is, four o'clock in the morning and finally I'm turning the last page.

And do you know what old Flick says to me then? He says, "Pammy, that is trash. You're reading trash."

What did he want from me? I'd given him a kid, a really neat kid. I'd groomed her to look like a movie star. I'd kept my figure, the hardest thing I'll ever have to do in my whole life. I mean, doesn't he think maybe I'd like a big fat slice of pie sometimes? Doesn't he think I don't dream night after night about fat old Mary Louise Palance and how maybe it would be nice to just say screw it like she did and balloon up into an old warthog myself? Doesn't he see I've fulfilled all my wifely duties up to and including you know what, I'll tell you what, screwing him anytime he wants, even though he doesn't ever want to anymore. Which I can hardly understand. Because standing here looking at myself in the mirror, a man would have to be hard put to find a reason not to want to just keep me in bed.

Flick's reasoning was this. He wanted me to read this book of poetry. If I could read it, he said, we'd bond together again, man and wife. So. I'm like, okay. Most women will do what it takes, learn that god-awful football or something. I figured I could learn to read his favorite book of poems and enjoy them, right? But do you think I could follow that crap? You've got to be kidding. I couldn't make out the first line. In the first place, I thought it was supposed to be about something. I'm not so dumb that I thought it had to rhyme or anything. Hell, I knew better than that. But at least it should be about something: "Leather nights and lentils Moon weeping sweeps Clinging, sighing, crying, dying." I mean, really.

I told him, "Flick, I love it. This is the best stuff."

You should have seen his face! That smile! Eureka! I had found the ticket! My marriage was saved! He got up from where he was sitting and grabbed me the way he used to do, dipping me and twirling me around the kitchen and we were happy again. Like how happy we were when he was in sales. When we still lived back in South Carolina, in a two story brick house with a circle driveway and Evie in a private school. Then he stopped and looked at me with these joyful tears in his eyes and he began questioning me about what I thought the poet meant by this and that.

I stood before him, blank. Doomed. Alone. Unlovable.

And then Audrey the coed bitch starts showing up with her perfect timing to talk to Flick about these very same books of poems and I knew I was in trouble.

She started out by borrowing them. Then she'd come by with all these questions for Flick to answer. Before long he was tutoring her at night, and I knew I should have been happy it was in our living room and not in his office with the door locked, and at first I was. But then I began to notice that Flick's strong arm of love around my shoulder was going slack when she showed up; and he was leaning so far over on the sofa that all I got to see of him anymore when that little bitch came over was the back of his head and his brand new wing tipped graduate shoe. His right one. His left one was always tucked on toe point like a hundred yard dash man ready to lift him off the couch at a moment's notice every time she laughed or breathed or looked like she might need a little teeny weeny little glass of water.

God. All the signs were there, plain as day, and me, like a stupid idiot, thinking, "So what if he flirts a little. A man's got to flirt. You cannot deny a man that. But he will never screw out on the beauty queen. And if he did, he would certainly never do it with Audrey." Which is one of the reasons I let her in my house in the first place. You learn to do that at an early age. Don't ever let a woman near who will outshine you. Surround yourself with dogs and the world is your banana and all that crap. Follow the book of rules.

And I did. But where has it all gotten me? My whole world is falling apart. And look at my little daughter, turning thirteen soon, growing chunky from unhappiness and biting her fingernails to the quick and I'm on her back and I can't get off it to save my life and I'm wondering, "Is this the way my mother felt when she rode my back with all the nagging?" And why can't I see why I can't stop? Why can't I see anything clearly anymore? Why is it that all I can see is my mother in me and me in my daughter?

God, I see myself in Evie all up and down. Like all that time I thought I was so weird cutting up Barbie's clothes and trying to find ways to get her unbendable legs to give way and wrap around Ken's. Those dolls were just screaming to be screwed. I'd spend hours trying to work it out. Hours. And I'd have the best time even though I knew I was heading straight for hell. But I didn't care. I was just so horny! There wasn't room for anything else. It was just me and Barbie and my raging hormones. And now my little girl comes along after all these years to show me just how normal it all was. And she's probably wondering right now just how messed up she is.

God, if I look back on everything, me and Flick and all

the things we've made it through, and how he's probably going to up and leave me, well, even adding that in the pot, I'd have to say that being thirteen was still the worst year of my life.

Poor old Evie. I want to pick her up in my arms and say, "Oh sweetie, it's okay if you want Ken and Barbie to screw. Everyone wants Ken and Barbie to screw. What else are you supposed to do with them?" But I can't say anything like that because I know if my mother had ever said something like that to me, I would have died right there on the spot. Not that Miss New Jersey would have ever said anything like that to me in a million years.

Evie's Barbie dolls have certain advantages mine did not. For instance, hers have bendable legs now. Everything bends. Her waist, her wrists, even her ankles. And Barbie has Jacuzzis and horse stables and waterbeds and beach houses and hair dryers and hair that grows and shortens up and can be brushed with Barbie's complete comb and brush set only after using Barbie's very own special shampoo, of course, and still, still there's nothing to do with her but make her screw old Ken.

Ken. Now there is a concept for you. Frankly I always thought he was such a drip. And Midge with that flat brown hair wasn't much either. And what happened? I married a Ken and now he's about to run off with a Midge and they may good and well deserve each other, the bores, but I've never been so lonely in my life.

Evie knows too. She's gone and cut all Midge's hair off and dressed her in another doll's clothes. She didn't have any Barbie outfits that weren't all cut to shreds so she took Raggedy Ann's apron and wrapped it around and around Midge and jammed Midge inside Barbie's wardrobe. Then she stuck Ken and Barbie in the beach house, side by side, holding hands and forever looking at what's ahead of them.

This is so sad. I find this so sad. She may not know she's done this. But I am this little girl's mother and I can tell you right now, for a cold hard fact, my little girl knows what's going on between her mommy and daddy.

And God, all I can do about it is stand here petrified before my mirror wondering when I started wearing my mother's shoes.

2

Y ou know what gets me about that woman? Audrey, that adulterating coed bitch, that's who I'm talking about. Okay. Well. There I am, carting my little beauty queen kid from town to town to town, staying at ratty motels to save Flick money, and meanwhile, he's got *her* holed up at our very own downtown Hyatt Regency ordering smoked salmon appetizers and bottled water. Yep. Bottled damned water and I'm drinking straight tap out of a cracked plastic cup worrying if they've got the stupid Disney Channel so my little Evie won't have a cow.

There's Flick, going on and on about how he can't support his little girl in the pageant world anymore. His little pride and joy. Well, I'm like, what the hell does he mean, because we've got a savings account the size of China. But ever since we'd moved to Atlanta and he'd started back to school, he was very sensitive about touching those savings and spending that money, so I said, "Okay, Flick. Calm down. Don't get all excited. We'll cut back." So Evie and I go from staying at these really swank hotels to staying at hotels where you don't have to worry about tipping a porter, but you can pretty much assume there's still going to be those little thingys, like miniature shampoo bottles and shoe horns, waiting for you in the bathroom right next to a stack of plush towels.

But then Flick says to me, "Pammy, things just can't keep on the way they're going. We're going broke." So the plush towels changed into not so plush ones with strings hanging off of them and we weren't walking through the lobby anymore. Instead we drove straight up to our room, looked both ways and ran as fast as we could to unlock the door so a rapist wouldn't abduct us.

Then one morning Flick's sitting at the kitchen table again with his head in his hands and his elbows on his books and he says, "Pammy, I know you love doing these shows. I know they're your life, but hon, the bills are killing me."

So I said, "But Flick, we're bringing home prize money. Evie's winning something every time."

Which wasn't exactly true. I mean, she wasn't exactly breezing through puberty like cute little Macayla Irvin who didn't even know what a pimple was. But I'd sneak some money out of our savings account and lay it on the table in front of his face whenever Evie lost a competition to make him think she'd won.

And that little girl. Do you think she has any damn sense? No. There I'd be, trying to keep her in crowns and her daddy happy and she's sulking by my side because I'm lying to him.

Well, you can't make everyone happy. And I'm beginning to think you can never make your own daughter happy. But if I thought there had been a chance in hell to make Flick happy I would have done anything.

Anything.

I even went so far as to go from sort of plush towels with strings hanging off, to flimsy towels that were so thin you could sift flour through them. They were no bigger than the paper bathmats. No bigger than the air conditioner, which I had to stand on a chair to get to in order to reach the control knobs. And still, still Flick kept coming at me with his long face and another stack of due bills.

Meanwhile, every other beauty queen's mother is staying at some fancy dancy hotel getting her daughter's gowns dry-cleaned. And there I am, washing Evie's gowns in the sink by hand and drying them with her hair dryer. And of course I'd have to make this big deal about pulling out a book of matches I'd swiped from the bathroom of the Radisson Town House to light my cigarette so this or that mother would think we were staying there. And I don't even smoke. But I tell you, it's enough to make a woman smoke.

So, I'm working like some dog trying to get my girl crowned around the region so she can move up on a national scale. And the big one is up. The big contest before she leaves Little Miss Junior Miss to go on to the Miss Teen. This time we're in Charlotte, North Carolina, staying in some fleabag next to a room full of construction workers and hookers with six-packs making a lot of noise. There is no Disney Channel. However, there are porn stations up the whazoo. I mean, I didn't pay much attention at first. But I run out to get some ice and when I come back, Evie's watching you-know-what all over the screen and I am horrified. And okay, any twelve-year-old is going to be fascinated with sex, but I was so angry about everything that once I started yelling, I couldn't stop. It just came pouring out. All of my frustrations with Flick just poured

out right on top of her little beauty queen head, only instead
of yelling about that son of a bitch, which is what I should
have been doing, I'm asking her how she can get so damned
fat on a diet? Did she not think I had eyes in my head? Did
she think I didn't see her thighs exploding into the size of
Flick's mother's? Should I just start calling her little fatso
now so she could get used to it when the time came, which,
by the way, wasn't so far off young lady?

And okay it was mean. But then she starts yelling back at
me! Well, I didn't need that. It was the first time she had
ever done that. The first time coming into thirteen had
reared its ugly head. And the fighting was on. Some creep
next door kept pounding on the wall until finally, exhausted,
Evie and I just ended up going to sleep. With our backs to
each other. Under the thinnest sheets God ever made.

The next morning we got up and went down to the show
as if nothing was wrong. Only something was wrong. The
invisible guillotine had dropped. The mother-daughter bond
had been broken. I knew it would take years to build back
up. I knew sometimes, like in the case with Miss New
Jersey and me, that bond wouldn't fuse back together until
one of us was dying. I thought about this as I watched my
little Evie up on stage. For someone who had spent the
entire night screaming about not wanting to be a beauty
queen anymore, she was giving it her all. She was knocking
the judges' socks off. One thing about my Evie, she is so
damned good in her talent spots it makes you want to cry.
This time she sang a hymn, "I Come to the Garden Alone."
You can always count on singing a hymn in Charlotte.
Unlike most places these days, Charlotte has some common
sense.

The Little Miss Junior Miss crown was practically on her
head. All she had left to do was her interview. The question

was, "If you had a million dollars, what would you spend it on?"

I'm sitting there thinking, piece of cake, because I had coached Evie on this exact question. "Come on, baby," I'm yelling in my head. "You've been trained. Say charity, Evie. Charity." Finally it's her turn. She steps up to the judge. She doesn't touch her face or do any rocking back and forth on the balls of her feet, thank God, but something's wrong. She's not talking. She's just standing there not saying a word. So there I am again, waving frantically to her not to blow it, and suddenly she starts bawling, "If I had a million dollars I'd get my daddy to come back home."

It was only later when I realized that she'd known all along what was going on between me and Flick. At the time, though, all I could think about was that the little brat was trying to get me back for the fight we'd had in the motel. I mean Flick hadn't exactly left, not physically anyway, so why else would she have said something like that except out of spite. I had to pull out two hundred dollars from our savings account for that little answer.

"We won! We won!" I came in smiling so fakely my teeth hurt. Flick was studying at the table. Evie was behind me crying.

"Why are you crying, sweetheart?" he asked her.

I squeezed the back of her neck to let her know I'd snap it in two if she even gave a hint, and I said, "She's just exhausted, Flick. We've got to get our little beauty queen to sleep."

So I put her to bed and the highlights that followed went something like this. I walked downstairs. Flick had stepped out. He was on the back porch smoking a cigarette. And then I noticed something strange. The washing machine was

going. Well, Flick doesn't wash clothes. In my whole
thirteen years of being married to him I'd never known him
to even load the dryer. So of course I'm scared he's mixed
his jeans in with my bra and panties. I rush to check on this
and sure enough there are blues and blacks mixed in with
whites so I get to work sorting things out. And then, lucky
for me, I remember to check my sweet husband's pockets
because the poor thing isn't going to know to take things out
of them.

I pull out this long, long, long hotel bill. It is wet. It is
wet but it is clear to me that there is a "2" under the
number of guests visiting. And it is clear to me that the card
number on the receipt is the very same MasterCard number
that I'd been using at all those fleabags. And it is clear to
me that Flick's signature is Flick's signature, because it's in
Flick's usual hieroglyphics. But what is not clear to me, and
only because it takes my entire life flashing before my eyes
for it to register, is all the things that have been run up on
this bill, dated three days ago when Flick was supposed to
be out of town on a young poets' conference. Dated three
days ago for the Hyatt Regency in this very town of Atlanta,
Georgia that we live in, was a bill for a $2.50 Butterfinger.
A damned candy bar. There was also steamed asparagus for
$6.50, an $8.00 hamburger and I will not even get into the
things that go over $20.00 except to say that there was some
kind of something on that bill called a Marie Brizzard for
about $46.00 and I do not even know what that is, but for
all I know or care it's some Swedish woman coming up to
join in all the fun.

And there's me and Evie, trying to figure out how to turn
on the Magic Fingers for a quarter and then spending the
rest of the night trying to figure out how to turn it off. Now,
I ask you, how do you bring this up with your husband?
How would you even begin? It is just too ridiculous for

words. So instead I took the bill and put it back in his pants pockets and stuffed all his colors back in with my white bras and panties and turned the washing machine back on. And the thumping, thumping of the machine matched the thumping, thumping of the headache that rose behind my eyes while I sat down at my little kitchen table and watched Flick out the kitchen door smoking his cigarette, thinking about the same thing I was thinking about. That coed bitch, Audrey, in bed with him.

3

Where the hell have I been? I should have known all along what was happening. Maybe it's not as simple as this—but I'm not so sure it's all that complicated either—but up until Audrey the slut came along, I could pretty much place Flick's bad moods in one of two categories: financial or health. So it didn't really make any sense when he started coming home and throwing his briefcase all over the place at the slightest thing I said. He'd just had a physical for school and his health was good. It couldn't have been that. And our bank account was in terrific shape. I mean, I'm talking about a man who had been so good at sales that when the trickle-down theory was in effect, if you were under Flick you were pretty much out of luck because nothing was going to be trickling down from him. Without exactly being a miser, he had managed to hold on to almost everything. When he decided to tear us out of our nice comfortable South Carolina home so he could go back to school in Atlanta, well, we could have afforded something a lot better than the dinky condo we got. But that's Flick for you. Always with his eye on the buck. He figured if he wasn't going to work, we should be safe and step down a notch. So, in great Flick style, we ended up stepping down two notches. No, three. I mean, okay, maybe we still had an upstairs and a downstairs, but if I stood in our combination living room/dining room and spread my arms, I could practically touch the grass wallpaper on both walls. All I'm saying is, a man like Flick doesn't let go of a penny without it taking some kind of toll.

So, with good health and a savings account, what was with the strained stuff? What was with all this snapping at me? What was with the new thing he had going, finishing all my sentences for me as if we were in some kind of race? What was with all the pacing? Jesus, the pacing. All the signs were there as plain as the pea green carpet that I couldn't stand, which I was standing on, and me standing on it not seeing a damn thing! I can just hear Miss New Jersey now, saying, "What are you, stupid?" And I would have to raise my hands in surrender and say, "Guilty. Take me in."

Just as I had stored away "pick up dry cleaning," "call about shoes," "get Evie's portfolio updated," I had found a safe little niche in my mind for "find out why Flick is more tense than he's ever been in the entire thirteen years, ten months and two weeks I've been married to him." It was just one of those things that you think you will get around to, but months later something comes along to remind you that you never did.

That hotel receipt was my little something.

And what I'd like to know, what I'd like for somebody to jump out of thin air and explain to me, please, is this. How come before I saw that receipt, I thought, "If Flick ever,

ever, *ever* has an affair on me, I will leave him." But after I saw it, I thought, "Please, please, please, Flick, do what you want but don't ever leave me."???

I wanted to take him in my arms and say, "Oh, Flick. It's okay if you want to have an affair. All men want to have an affair. You want to stay young. You don't want to die. Nobody expects you to be monogamous." But I couldn't say that. For one thing, I did expect him to be monogamous. For another, I'd be an idiot to say something like that. Saying something like that would just set him up to say, "Pammy, this is thoughtful of you, but I don't want an affair. I want a divorce so I can marry Audrey the coed tramp slut."

Somehow I just felt there was safety in not bringing it up at all. If I mentioned it, Flick's and Audrey's names would be carved in stone forever. There'd be no sucking it back. But if I kept my mouth shut, the whole, awful, tiresome affair would be like the smoke that rose from Flick's cigarette as he stood outside and thought of her—something he took in and I only had to catch a glimpse of. Eventually, it would drift away with the wind and vanish.

Of course, not mentioning it didn't mean I had to sit around like a damned patsy and watch the world go by. Watch him go off on another one of those mysterious trips he was always going to so much trouble to keep me from going on.

This isn't what I was used to. This isn't the way my marriage was supposed to turn out. I thought it was going to be the screen door slamming every night behind Flick with him so happy to see me, kissing my neck, asking what was for dinner. And if he did go on a trip, he'd always take me. He always used to take me. For the first four months before I got pregnant, and most of the nine when I was, he wouldn't have dreamed of going off on one of his sales trips without me. And as soon as Evie was old enough to take along, we'd be off again. If he had business in Florida, he'd make sure we'd go to Disney World. If it was in Atlanta, he'd take us to Six Flags. There wasn't one place he wanted to go without us. Then school started for Evie and sometimes we couldn't go. But he'd always call two or three times a day and say he wished we were there.

And then school started for Flick. Business ended. But he kept going on trips. Trips which at first he said were to collect old commissions from his sales job. He still called me two and three times a day to tell me exactly where he was and what he was doing, or what he thought I ought to be thinking he was doing. He'd even tell me the next time he went somewhere he was going to bring me along. Then those three calls dropped to two and then to one and then to none.

I mean, you don't know. You bitch a little bit—where's my call and all that nagging, and you do nag—but dammit, sometimes a woman just gets tired of nagging, of bitching. She sits by the phone and waits for the calls that never come and watches her child grow, and somewhere along the line she leaves the phone. She just gets so damn tired of asking so many damn questions. And I did get tired of it. Lord, I got so tired of it. I said to myself, "Stop, Pammy. Just stop." I mean, it's just easier to think that if you're being faithful to your husband and keeping your figure and telling him everything that is going on in your life, then surely he's going to be doing the same thing. Right?

Well, I am here to tell you, it doesn't always work out that way.

I remember when I first realized this. I was standing in my kitchen slapping down two slices of bread, as if they were playing cards, for Evie's peanut butter sandwich, and I was listening to Flick telling me that, once again, he was going out of town to collect a couple of outstanding commissions.

I was like, "Okay, Flick if you say so, but since you don't work anymore, can't they just mail them to you or something?"

He rolled his eyes, "Oh, Pammy. It doesn't work that way." He then explained to me how it did work as I spread Evie's favorite peanut butter—Skippy Super Chunk—trying desperately to believe him, and by the time I'd smoothed it into the corners and scraped it off the crust I did believe him. I even sent him on his way with all my love and a kiss.

But then when I went back inside and took up where I'd left off—smoothing grape jelly just right so when Evie inspected her sandwich later it would be exactly the same amount on every spot of bread—I got the phone call. The one that caught Flick Outlaw in a red-handed lie big enough to walk. It wasn't a business call. It wasn't a call from a client. It was the host of the Young Poets of North Georgia, reminding Flick that they were meeting up in the mountains for their annual writers' retreat that very weekend.

Well, I figured it must be a mistake. Something he could clear up with his next phone call home. But that phone call never came. All weekend it didn't come. And I went from holding loneliness at arm's length, watching it, studying it, wondering what it was going to do to me if it invaded my body, to softly bringing it in and fitting it into my one little lonely breaking heart. It was the first time I'd ever been lonely in my marriage to Flick. It was more lonely than all the lonelinesses I'd ever been through even before I was married.

By the time Flick got back home and stood at the kitchen door, I'd gone through a thousand scripts. I'd say this, I'd say that. But in the end I settled on the truth. "You lied to me, Flick. You didn't go on any business trip. You went on a retreat.''

And do you know what he did? Do you know what that husband of mine did? Probably what every man who is ever caught in a lie does. He just looked at me blank faced and said it was still a business trip and he walked off.

It was right in there when I got the hot flash that told me exactly how much brains he thought I had.

I carefully made Evie another peanut butter and jelly sandwich and squared the top slice of bread and put the lid on the Skippy and the Bama sugar-free jelly and put the bread away and tried to figure out what I was going to do next.

Well, eventually I did what any normal red blooded woman would do. I left it up to my feelings and it wasn't long before I was tearing up the stairs after him, flying back down the stairs following him, screaming at him. And then he was screaming at me. Up until then we had always kept our fights in the bedroom. But this was the first time we had let one rip through the house, and there's my little Evie, sitting quietly at the dining room table pretending to do her homework, pretending not to hear. Her sandwich was left untouched.

I don't remember how long that fight lasted, but eventually I became too tired not to want to believe the great big lie Flick told me. Some crap about how he didn't want to alarm me about spending money instead of making it. And me like a stupid idiot thinking, "So, what if he lied. He didn't want to. A man like that must be feeling an awful lot of pressure from his wife to have to go and lie like that." And I promised myself that I would never ever put Flick in one of those spots again.

After that, we just sort of fell into a pattern. He'd drive off to a writers' workshop somewhere, and Evie and I would stay home and play house and usually he'd forget to call. It never occurred to me, or maybe I just didn't want it to occur to me, why he no longer invited us to come along.

It just never occurred to me that he'd let somebody else take our place.

I hated Macayla Irvin and her mother was trash, but sometimes there are worse things than trash. Such as seeing that your husband's bags are packed again, ready to go, and there you are about to let him leave. Even after he's gotten sloppy enough to let you find out he's having an affair. No. No way. That hotel receipt was my flashing red light. The lying and hiding and cheating and humming and dressing up and slapping on extra Old Spice were a pleasure compared to the evidence which I had pulled out of my washing machine. Well, I may not have known much, but I knew when it got to the point where Flick was sloppy enough for me to find him out, then it was time to make a move.

So the next day I stuck Evie at Macayla's trashy house so I could work on getting my husband back. I had to answer all kinds of nosey questions Amanda Irvin asked about why we were going off in the middle of the week and how long we were going to be gone, with all kinds of lies about a dying uncle, because frankly, I had no idea how long we were going to be gone. I mean, Flick didn't even know I was going to go yet. Actually, I didn't even know where we were going. I was just swirling around in Flick's great adulterating vortex without a clue.

I knew Amanda Irvin would feed Evie candy bars until she threw up, while her precious little Macayla ate salads and sulked. I had pulled this same trick a number of times myself. But that was because I had had a reason. While Evie's cute little girlish figure was just inches away from not being so cute anymore, that little Irvin slut was perfect regulation size beauty queen. Pftttt. I spit on her.

"I thought you hated Macayla," Evie said, as I packed her overnight bag.

"I don't hate Macayla, honey. I just hate her mother. Now go change. There's a nice little outfit lying on Mommy's bed for you to wear."

I knew what would come next. I clamped my jaw and waited for the explosion.

"Why do I have to wear this?! I'm not wearing this!" Evie came wailing back down the hall. She stood before me, still wearing her black everything. Black T-shirt. Black Lycra pants. Black cowboy boots. Her daddy's black bowler hat. She looked like a fucking morgue. "I am sleek and fast like a bullet," she said, sticking her chin out defiantly, throwing the dress on the floor. "You cannot make me change."

I virtually ripped those clothes off my screaming child and whipped her into a little number Amanda Irvin would die for. A snazzy red dropwaist with rhinestones on the hem, which Miss New Jersey had Federal Expressed straight from a New York City showroom. Of course, Evie wouldn't quit crying, so I had to give her twenty dollars to shut her up. "Get over it," I said, as I yanked her little red panty hose up a little higher. "If you let that woman know you've been crying I will wring your neck. There, there. Mommy's going to take you to a nice movie when we get back from our vacation."

God, I love my little girl. She has the sweetest skin. I didn't want to yell at her. I didn't want to make her cry. I wanted to lie down beside her and trace my fingers around her face and neck and stomach and marvel at how she was mine, the way I used to do when she was a baby and things weren't so messed up around here. But that time had passed. I was lucky if I could get a hug from her these days. So, I went about my business and packed all her black clothes in a black box and stuck them into the blackest part of the closet, for life. Then I drove up to the Irvins' where they had a big brick two story and a circle driveway like we used to have, and I let her out. She didn't even look at me as she walked away. And the back of her neck looked exactly like the back of Flick's neck when he walked away.

Did these people not see they were breaking my heart? Had I been breaking my mother's heart the same way? Sometimes I thought I'd just have to grab my head to keep it from falling off from the pain of all the worrying and thinking and mulling things over. I was a factory of thoughts. And it wasn't like all the thinking ever did me any good either. I never came to a conclusion or solved anything. The truth of the matter was, once I got started shaking myself up over one thing, three more things came along to do me in; it was a chain reaction from hell.

Sometimes a woman can get so damned tired of thinking so much. Sometimes a woman just wants to dress up and be pretty and see where that will take her. So when Flick came whistling across the lawn, tossing the keys of his brand new Chrysler convertible in the air, I poofed out my yellow sundress and put on my best beauty queen smile.

He twirled around, twice, laughing to himself. Laughing! Then he saw me and his face dropped into the last century. "Where do you think you're going?" he snapped.

"With you, sweetie," I flirted. I felt like sandpaper flirting.

"Where's Evie?" He didn't look at me, but when I told him where she was, he said the same thing she had said. "I thought you hated Macayla Irvin?"

"Whatever gave you that idea, Flick?" I smiled and patted the driver's seat. "Come on, let's go. We haven't been anywhere together in a long, long time."

What could he do? He got in and turned the engine on.

Then he turned it back off and hit the dashboard hard and told me to wait because he had to make a quick phone call. Well, any idiot could see he had to call Audrey the coed tramp slut and tell her not to hold her bitchy breath waiting for him because she wasn't going anywhere. She was going to have to stay right where she was, at her crummy little duplex thinking about him in bed with me for a change.

I must have sat in that car, under that hot May sun, for forty minutes, while he smoothed her rumpled slut feathers. When he finally got back in, beat down, I wanted to rake his cheating eyes out. But that was for another time. This was a time for getting him back.

We went to Charleston. I'd never been to Charleston before but it was everything I had ever imagined it would be. The place sparkled! The houses were painted salt water taffy colors, and under the setting sun they looked like watercolor paintings. There were horse drawn carriages trotting up and down the streets. And beautiful trees, called palmetto trees, which looked like feather dusters lining the sidewalks. And I was thinking, "This is right. This is the way it should have been the whole damn time. Forget that he's lying. Forget that he's in love with another woman. The fact is, we are here now, husband and wife."

I didn't know who Flick's friends were. He'd never spoken of them before. But the minute he took the Charleston exit off I-26, he began filling me in on who they were and what I shouldn't say so I wouldn't embarrass him.

"Flick, I was fourth runner-up at the Miss America. I doubt I'm going to embarrass you," I snorted, amazed at even the idea.

What he didn't understand was, I wasn't going to do anything to put him out. For instance, the entire trip I had sat very still and listened to him not talk to me. Now that is not easy to do. To sit and stare at nothing, at hundreds of thousands of southern pines blurring off to your side, at one happy couple in the car passing you in the fast lane, while you sit quietly and pretend you are not straining to keep from lunging for the steering wheel so you can swerve the car off the side of the road and scream, "You filthy, rotten trash! Don't you see that you are ruining our lives!"

But there I sat, one lonely married woman, holding tons of adultery-hating energy at bay in my small 110-pound frame.

After about an hour of silent treatment, Flick popped a cassette into the player and we listened to a pretty good book about another lonely woman. Only in the end she jumps in front of a train. I must admit, I was very disappointed with that, but Flick sat back on his little beaded car seat and said the first thing he'd said to me the whole trip. "See, Pammy, that is what I call real literature."

Well, maybe, but frankly I prefer the books I read where in the end the woman gets the man and he screws her eyes out and they live happily ever after, because if you don't get that in books, you're sure as hell not going to get it in real life. You could tell that much just by looking at me and Flick.

4

I've never felt so out of place. The very moment Professor Smith-Krofton opened the front door to his huge historical pink house I knew I wasn't going to be welcome. The three or four people there before us circled quietly around me like shadows, whispering, trying to figure out who I was. And then Flick started walking two feet ahead of me as if he didn't know who I was! And he sat about eight feet away from me whenever we sat down.

Mostly we all stood in this great white kitchen with a big ceiling fan blowing the humidity around and around and talked about poetry and critical theory. Well, they talked. I listened. Well, I really didn't even listen, because I couldn't follow word one of what they were saying. And when they weren't talking about stuff I didn't understand, they were talking about people I didn't know.

And there's Flick. Standing over by the coffeemaker, sneering. I mean, my husband doesn't sneer. When did my husband start sneering? This was insane. And that's when I began to realize that my husband had been sneering all along.

Then everyone started to leave the kitchen—some to go to the porch, others to go to the living room—because they had all been there and they had all known each other and they all knew where to go. But me, like a stupid idiot with no place to go, just stood where I was pretending to read a damn newspaper clipping that was pinned on the refrigerator by a plain magnet. Not a magnet shaped like a banana or a milkshake or a bird or a fish or something you'd like to reach up and touch, but a plain old boring magnet holding up an incredibly boring article about taxes, entitled "Audited! Audited! And Audited Again!" And whenever anyone walked in, I started reading it from the beginning again, as if it were the most interesting thing I had ever read in my entire life. As if I could not learn enough about discriminant functions and compliance measurement programs. I mean, really.

By the time Professor Smith-Krofton came back in it was pitch dark outside and I'd read that article maybe five times and understood none of it. He opened the refrigerator, knocking me out of my little space, my little safe territory, and he had the nerve to ask me if I'd gotten anything out of that stupid article.

"Why yes!" I beamed.

Then he sort of laughed and pulled out some cheeses and began slicing them up and said, "So, David tells me you're a beauty queen?"

Well, sorrrry, but it just didn't sound like a question. It sounded more like an insult. And by the way, I'm thinking, when did everyone start calling Flick David? It was then that I began to realize these people had been calling him David all along.

A glass of wine was poured and someone said, "Let's have a toast for David." Someone mixed a plate of chips and pesto and it was, "Here David, you Deconstructionists need all the nourishment you can get." The phone rang and not only did David dash to the kitchen to pick it up, but Professor Smith-Krofton grabbed it first, nodded my way and said, "David, it's for you. You want to take it in the bedroom?" And there I was, reading that fucking article again.

Who would ever have thought I would end up being a stranger in my own marriage? It was one thing for Flick and Audrey to lie in bed and talk about him divorcing me—and I'm not so stupid to think they hadn't. I could look at these people and tell they had. That was the thing. You see, adulterers can believe anything when they talk about it in bed. But somewhere down the line Flick had taken it out from under the covers and made it real to these people, and it had taken me standing in that kitchen not moving around them while they moved around me, to see that they were not about to invest any time in getting to know who I was because I wasn't going to be around long enough to be known. They were not even going to take the pains to learn my name. To these people, I was always going to be "her," soon to be replaced by a newer, brighter one of "them."

5

If I had a million dollars I would pay someone to make me smart enough to talk to Flick. Supposing I did want to ask him what the hell he thought he was doing with Audrey? He would only start in with that crazy critical theory stuff. And once he started in with that I would be completely defenseless. You see, he had learned to say just about anything he wanted, do anything anytime he wanted, anyway he wanted to do it because he had discovered the fine art of boiling just about everything he did down to an exact justification of his actions.

He called it critical theory. I called it crap.

For instance, a few months ago, before I even knew that any of this was going on, I wanted to get a fish tank and some angel fish. Evie's so allergic to dogs and cats and lately she'd been acting so damned allergic to me that I just needed to have some kind of company. Something. Anything to cure the horrible loneliness that had dug its nails into my back. But Flick? Flick had said, "No, Pammy. No fish. Who's going to feed them?"

As if I were a child. As if I had not fed him and my daughter breakfast, lunch and dinner for the past thirteen years world without end. And many times lately, even I don't know how many, his mistress. I mean, I was mad. So I told him, "Flick, I'm mad. This really pisses me off."

So he put his arm around me and started in with that junk. "Let me ask you something, Pammy. What is the point of a fish tank, really?"

"The point is, I want one."

"Well, no," he said. "That's not the point at all. Actually, to comprehend the point you have to separate yourself from the tank. You have to delve further. Think about the fish. The bubbles. The colored gravel. The plantlife. New Criticism would say that it's the whole picture itself that is the point and that I'm here to tell you that."

"What?"

"However, that would be disqualifying the significance of the air around the tank and the air inside the tank."

"What's the point here, Flick?"

"That's it, Pammy! That's exactly it!" He was getting excited. You can always tell when Flick's excited because he spreads his fingers and it sort of looks as though he's dribbling these imaginary basketballs. "The panes of glass separate the water from the air. The tank would not be, would not exist, without the glass. And since there needs to be something that separates the fish from us, that something, that loss, if you will, is created by the glass. So, in essence, the glass itself is the point of the fish tank. That's what the Deconstructionist would say."

Suddenly I was thinking, who is this jerk? What the hell is he talking about? It was then that I realized Flick had been a Deconstructionist all along. Turning everything into a major breakthrough into the obvious. A major breakthrough into pure, unadulterated bullshit. A major breakthrough into who cared. "Flick," I said. "All I want is some damn fish. I don't give a rat's ass what the point is."

"Pammy, I'd rather you not get that fish tank until you can start learning the significance of learning."

What the hell, so I got the fish tank anyway. And the fish, Sam, Gretel, Gertrude and Beatrice. Evie named them. And the gravel and the plantlife and I even got a catfish that sucked the algae off the sides of the glass itself, and two guppies, which was a big mistake, because they immediately had tons of babies, ate them and ended floating belly up on top of the water. Not something I wanted my little Evie to see. But not once, not one damn time, did I ever lose any sleep over what the point of my new fish tank was. But it was right around that time when I began to wonder what the point of my husband was.

And standing in that Charleston kitchen where all Flick's friends had finally come in to talk to me, I began to wonder what the point of anything was. They were not there to talk to me out of politeness. They were there to talk to me because Flick was upstairs committing adultery all over their phone and they wanted to buy him time. I may have been stupid for marrying him, but I was no idiot. I was not about to run upstairs and cause a scene the way Miss New Jersey would probably have done. What those people did not know was that I had spent my entire life trying not to be my mother and the last thing I was going to do was start being her now. I was going to stay right where I was, pinned against the refrigerator with them leaning forward with all this fake interest, asking me about the pageant world.

I began talking. Suddenly I was up on that stage at the Miss America when Bert Parks first walked out. He was looking directly at me, a surefire sign that I was the winner.

I told them exactly what it felt like to be standing on that Atlantic City stage as one of the top five contestants, waiting for my title to be announced. My pulse was beating on the left side of my neck; a hole had opened all the way from my throat to my stomach where I was dropping my breath to keep from squealing; my panty hose had ridden up the crack of my butt; all that and then my name was the first name called. Not the last name, the Miss America title. No, I was called to accept the fourth runner-up title. The other girls had to push me to cross the stage to take my small bunch of flowers. Small compared to the explosion of roses I'd been practicing to carry down the runway for so many weeks, months, years.

I was just getting to that part when Professor Smith-Krofton interrupted and said, "No. No. David said you had some really great stories. What it was like backstage with all the catfighting and backstabbing. You know. Those stories."

I stared at him. It wasn't like that at the Miss America. Where did he get such an idea? What was he talking about? We had a great time in Atlantic City. We were like sisters there. And then it dawned on me. Flick had told them my stories about the other pageants. The ones that had made him laugh so long ago when he said that I had the best sense of humor in the world. When he said that he was so in love with me that if he didn't snatch me up to be his wife, someone else was going to come along and take me away. Those were the times when everything was our little secret, when he taught me all about laughing at the sad things, the bad things, the embarrassing things, about laughing at myself.

But now it was no longer me making fun of me. But them making fun of me. And that made all the difference. I wasn't about to tell them all my little secrets about spraying my rearend with hairspray to keep my swimsuit from riding up when I sweated. Or about that time I swiped Mary Louise Palance's hairspray and replaced it with a spray can of Pam cooking oil which I had dressed up to look like VO5, to get her back for that awful time she had put red dye in my bottle of Q-T so instead of having a kind of orangish tan on my legs, they looked scorched.

Then it came to me that, yes, maybe I ought to tell Flick's friends all the stories. Maybe I ought to tell them the ones about sleeping around with the judges. And just lately, loosening the heels on little Macayla Irvin's shoes at the Little Miss Junior Miss Pageant so that when she got up on stage they'd break, because I had figured out that she'd been sleeping with the woman judge who sold the expensive show gowns that you sort of either had to buy or you didn't have a damn chance. And I'd bought my little Evie's from her for a whopping eight hundred dollars only to find out that Macayla Irvin was going to win anyway and you bet I was going to do something to clock her ass. Imagine sleeping with a judge before your thirteenth birthday. At least that's what I'd heard anyway.

I thought about a lot of things in those next few seconds. I even thought about fat old Mary Louise Palance and how maybe I should break down and give that old girl a call to see what she was up to. Probably 250 pounds, bless her Jersey heart. And I thought about my mother, Miss New Jersey. She was probably, right now, trying to get her husband, Joe, to attend church. And he was probably trying to get her off his back so he could go hit a bucket of golf balls the way he had been doing every day since they'd been married. Married almost thirty years and Flick and I weren't even going to make it to our fourteenth.

Finally, in the end, it was the not being able to swallow that made me smile weakly and walk out the door without saying a word. And once I'd walked out one door, walking out the other door, the front door, and opening up my car door, was easy.

Every door was a gate to freedom. At that moment, nothing had ever felt quite so good as driving away from that house. From those people. If that was what the Old South was like, then it was a good thing Sherman had come through and burned most of it up. I didn't care that Charleston was made up of one-way cobblestone streets and I was always either going down the wrong one the right way or the right one the wrong way. It didn't even matter that it was about a seven-hour drive back home to Atlanta and it was already ten o'clock at night. Getting away from those people, I could have driven forever.

The radio was playing and it was playing my songs. All the oldies from the good old days, when life was great and Flick loved me and I actually got along with Miss New Jersey. "Can't Take My Eyes Off Of You" was blasting out and I was da-da-dahing because I never could get the words straight to a song. I was banging on the steering wheel, crying and laughing and saying, "God, I'm so glad I'm out of there. I am out of that house. *Daaa-daaa-daaa-da-da-da-daaaaaaa. Da-da-da-daaa-da-da-daaaaaaa.* I am out of that awful house. Flick, honey, I hate you, Flick. I hate you. I hate your friends!"

Out on the highway it began to rain and the windshield wipers picked up the beat of an old song that reminded me of a drunk woman I knew when I was a child. She was the mother of my first childhood friend. I'd go to that little girl's house because she had a record player. We'd always put on the forty-five of "Love Is Blue." Those were the days when you still had to fit a little red plastic ring over the spindle so the forty-five wouldn't go flying around like a warped pot on a potter's wheel. The music would come pouring out, making me feel so good that I'd just have to sing along. And every time I sang, my friend's mother would come in and sit on the edge of the white canopy bed and ask me to sing it again. She'd pull me over and make me stand straight and tall, placing my six-year-old hands and feet just so, and I'd sing for her. I'd sing my little heart out. I didn't really know what the words meant, but I knew what the music meant. It meant the same for me that it meant for her. That my daddy had left me, just like her husband was leaving her. And as I sang about that, tears would stream down her cheeks, and when the song was over, she'd point her glass of gin at me and say, "One more time, honey." And I'd sing that song so many times that finally one day I realized that my daddy was never coming home but my mother was always home and I was just too young to be that sad. So I quit going over there altogether.

Later I won the Little Miss Apple Tree singing that same song at the New Jersey Apple Festival, but that's not what I thought about whenever I heard that song. I always thought about that old drunk woman sitting on that little girl's white canopy bed.

The rain let up and I picked up speed and passed a slow truck. I wondered about that woman now. I never thought about her daughter, but a lot of days, and almost every day since Flick and I had been breaking up, I'd thought about the woman and wondered if she still drank and still took those pills and still screamed at other little girls the way she had screamed at me when I wasn't singing to her; screamed, why was I making her go so crazy? And had those other little girls stood with their hands in their pockets wondering why they were so bad? And had those same girls grown up and left that neighborhood and left New Jersey and were now on some rainy highway wondering, as I was wondering, why their husbands were leaving them?

A funny thing about that woman. She had a beautiful house, a french poodle that was trimmed to show, a white Cadillac, an aunt who used to know Lucille Ball personally, and a husband who, although he was always at work, brought home gobs of money every week to keep her in booze and furs and pills and still, still, there was nothing for her to do but cry at me when I sang and scream at me when I didn't.

I think if somebody asked me what my biggest fear was, it would not be my husband leaving me. It would be me turning into a mean old lady. I mean, old ladies don't plan on turning out mean and paranoid and nasty, do they? It just happens, doesn't it? I think about my mother and how she locks up her pocketbook and silver and makeup so the maid won't steal from her even though the maid has been coming for thirty years and has never taken a dime. I think about my mother and how she goes out to lunch with her friends and comes home, taking off her summer gloves finger by finger without a kind word to say about the lot of them. I think about her and how she threw away some dresses instead of giving them to Josephine, her maid, because she didn't want any of her rich, country club friends to see her dresses being worn by a woman who isn't even seen anywhere except a small church and grocery store on the outskirts of town. And then I think, she didn't plan on being that way, did she? Surely it just snuck up on her. Just like that time snuck up on me in South Carolina when I cut down the pomegranate tree in my backyard because teenage boys were picking the fruit after school and eating it. Why, I ask myself over and over, did I do such a thing? And the answer is always the same scary answer: because I am my mother's daughter and if I couldn't eat that fruit then nobody else should. I used to put fertilizer around that same tree to try and make it grow back. When it did, I vowed never to eat its pomegranates again. I planned to give that fruit away to every boy who came by my house. I planned to do whatever it took to offset that horrible, terrible disease that roared towards me like a freight train—the virus of my mother's movements, which she had planted in me at birth.

I do not want to be the kind of old woman my mother is. I want to be charming and have little candy dishes all over my house. I want to wear white powder on my face and the back of my neck and have little girls look at me in the grocery stores and wish I were their grandmother. That is what I want.

But I tell you, you cannot have everything you want. You cannot even have your husband back when he leaves even though he is rightfully yours.

The windshield wipers squeaked across the windshield. I turned them off, but an irritating mist made me turn them right back on. I drove along, very depressed, listening to them squeak as my radials whistled down the wet road. Then some small-town deejay who was probably in a trailer behind a soybean field, unaware that he was about to break my heart, put on our song. Mine and Flick's. "This Guy's In Love With You." I started my da-dahing again as I pulled off the road, onto the shoulder under an overpass, and parked. It was just me and our song and the tree frogs all singing together after a southern rain. I got out and lay down on the hood of the car—I didn't care that it was wet—and wondered just where Flick and I would go from here. *Da-da da-da. Da-da da-da da daaa. Da-da da-da.* I wondered if it even mattered anymore? Then I figured, probably not. Because lying out there on that hood, looking at the fog blow past the stars, it occurred to me that you just can't spend a minute of your life with people who don't care a ding about you.

And then our song was over. A recap tire commercial

came belting out, jolting me out of my terrible thoughts. So I got back in the car, my back wet with the rain from the hood, and pulled out in the slow lane. And that song, "I Love You More Today Than Yesterday," came on and it came to me that yes, okay, it did matter. It mattered a great deal. He may not have been much, but he was my husband and I loved him and I was not ready to lose him. It was too late to turn back and get him, but I could certainly drive forward and get to Atlanta in time for breakfast. In time to pick up Evie. In time to see her sweet little face. And in her face I'd see Flick's face and mine, mixed together, staring up at me, watching me, trusting me to pull us out of this mess and bring us back together again. Somehow. Someway.

My little Evie's face. I could drive all night for my little Evie's face.

6

When I drove back into Atlanta, the sun was just coming up, first shining on Stone Mountain, then glinting off the copper Capitol dome. I'd driven all night. I was beyond tired. Something else had cut in—a new energy mixed in with the Beach Boys playing over the airwaves, telling me how I should dress and wear my hair and who I should hang out with. And I can't really explain it but I was making all these new resolutions: be a better wife, be a better mother, turn into something that one day my grandchildren can write an essay about for *Reader's Digest* and win a scholarship to college. Be the Pammy I used to be. The happy-go-lucky girl who could talk on the phone for hours with nothing to say. The girl who used to paint her toenails and walk around the house with cotton wedgies between her toes preparing for a date. The girl who used to date. The girl who used to have fun cleaning up, pretending that she was already married to a gorgeous handsome husband, instead of already married to one who had turned into a cad.

I don't know why, but I decided to wait to pick up Evie. I just wanted to go home and feel one of my beauty queen dresses sliding down my body again. I wanted to clean up my filthy condo. I wanted to bake some bread and iron all of Flick's clothes while I talked on the phone. It didn't have to make sense, it just had to make me feel good.

And suddenly I did feel good, like the Pammy I used to be. I did my full hair, my full makeup, painted my fingernails and toenails a soft petal pink, three coats, and walked around on my heels with the wedgies in place and decided that directly after I put on my Miss South Carolina gown, I'd give old Mary Louise Palance a call and catch up on the old times. That was what was missing for me: old times and girlfriends. I was whistling up the stairs. Whistling in the attic. Whistling as I unzipped the hanging storage bag and pulled out my gold lamé gown. Whistling as I pulled its silky fabric over my head. But then I stopped whistling.

The damned thing wouldn't zip up. Impossible.

We are talking about a woman who was not even as skinny as the day *before* she became pregnant, but a woman who was skinnier even than that! I was the same size as when I won the Miss New Jersey Teen. The year before I moved south and gained five pounds. And my dress wouldn't zip up? How was it possible?

I weighed myself. One hundred and ten pounds. Good.

I measured myself. Breasts: thirty-two. Thirty-two?! Good God! Waist: twenty-three. Twenty-three?! Jesus Christ! It was supposed to be twenty. I'd spent so much time on the scales keeping myself down to 110 pounds, that it never occurred to me those pounds might shift, change, drop! My breasts had turned into my waist, my waist had turned into my hips, God knows what my ass had turned into.

I left my clothes in a bundle on the floor and left the attic.
I was still wearing my gown, still unzipped, but I wasn't
thinking about it. I was thinking about Mary Louise. I really
needed to talk to her. See how she was. See if she ever
thought about me. See if she'd ever lost weight. I thought
about that all the time. I thought about her all the time. But
the reason I never called her was because, well, because she
was fat. And she wasn't just smooth fat, either. She looked
like one of those balloons that had been twisted around and
tortured into the shape of an animal. That kind of fat.
Dimpled at the joints. And I know it's horrible, but it just
bothered me so much. I think being around Mary Louise
Palance made me uncomfortable because when I looked at
her I saw myself.

See, somebody else might point out a slim, svelte, reed
of a woman strolling briskly through a mall and say, "Why,
Pammy, that's what you look like." But me, I'd search
around until I saw someone so heavy she had to stop every
fifty feet or so to catch her breath, and I'd say, "Nope.
That's me." Of course, everybody would then say, "Oh,
Pammy. You're just fishing for compliments." But they
wouldn't understand that I really, truly, honestly felt that
way. If you had a mother like mine, which I do, and have
ever gotten fat, which I did, then you will never remember a
time when you weren't, which I am, even if you are standing
skeletal before your own bedroom mirror. Someone might say,
"God, woman, you are too skinny," but what you will hear is
your mother saying, "Well, congratulations, Pammy, you've
gone up another size. My own little fatso."

She used to slap magic oils all over my legs, arms,
stomach, neck and then twirl Saran Wrap around me and
make me sit out in the hot sun for hours in order to reduce.
She put me on diet toast, diet meats, diet this, diet that,
grapefruit diets, low carb then high carb diets, no-mucus

diets. She saunaed me, steam bathed me, ran me up and down the Schoolhouse Lane hill so many times that eventually my leg muscles began to get too big and she had to quit. And then one day I woke up and I was the right weight, height, everything and the horror was over.

The only thing is, you never forget the horror.

I never forgot.

My hips feel as if they're spreading every time I look at a fashion model leaping across the TV set in a Diet Coke commercial. I look back at the pictures of myself during my fat stage and think, I wasn't fat. I was only fifteen or twenty pounds overweight, tops. So why do I only see flab, flab, giant mounds of flab? I see a fat person walking by my condo and I turn away because, well, because I don't know why. It doesn't make sense. Just as how fat I remain in my head, even today, up to and including this very day when I sat down at my own kitchen table, 110 pounds and unable to zip up my gown, doesn't make sense.

And now here I am, fifteen years later, turning every skinny inch of myself into my mother, putting my little girl through the same horror. Well, at least I let Evie eat peanut butter. My mother would never have let me eat peanut butter. My mother never even let me eat potatoes.

The phone rang at Mary Louise's Hackensack, New Jersey home a total of nine times before a man picked it up laughing. "Hello," he said, and I said, "Is Mary Louise there?" and he laughed and said, "Are you here, Mary Louise?" There was all this great tickling action and giggling and squealing, and then he came back on and said, "Yes. She's here but she can't come to the phone right now. Can I take a message?"

I hung up on him. I put my head on the table. I tried to cry, but couldn't. I threw my head back and made a weird throaty wail, trying to make myself cry. But even that didn't help. Nothing would come. I was beyond being miserable. I put my head on the table again and just lay there.

How could my life have come down to this? A woman who had fought all her life to stay slim, loses her man, while a woman who never fought at all, had found one? For as long as I could remember Mary Louise never had a boyfriend. Well, okay, she was married once, but that didn't count since he was a jerk. And I knew she was still fat because my mother had just recently bumped into her and called to tell me about it. She had said, "Pammy, she's bigger than a Cadillac. I told her I saw you a month ago and she asked what you were wearing. For fifteen years the girl hasn't seen you and the first thing she wants to know is what you're wearing. And you want to know what she's wearing? A sack, I'm telling you. A muumuu."

All of that weight on one ex-beauty queen and she still finds a man to love her. And me, a pencil thin, full grown lonely woman with no man. Was this my fate?

No. I had to believe there was a better answer than that. Maybe fate is where things will just happen to you if you don't make them happen for yourself. An example. There was a time when I felt Flick slipping away. This was years and years ago. But during that time my old friend, Chuck, a judge I hadn't slept with but who had been a good friend, called out of the blue. Chuck had the weirdest body, the weirdest baldness. The top of his head looked like chicken skin with a few tiny hairs sticking out. He wore his pants up to his armpits. He wore his shirt untucked and so thin you could see his pants through it. And if I'd brought him around to my house, Flick would have laughed. He was that unattractive. But I didn't have to let Flick know that. Flick had never met him before. So. I got off the phone and began acting different. Kind of coy. A little happier than normal. Just a little something to get the juices stirring again. That's when I found out the sad truth of it all . . . there is no love tempter stronger than the jealousy a wife can stir up in her husband. After that, I figured I would always mention Chuck if I ever felt Flick slipping away.

But then I had Evie and somehow it just didn't seem right anymore. All the games and there I was putting fresh, clean diapers on my little girl's tiny baby bottom with her smiling up at me, and it came to me that love was not trying to trick somebody, but trying to be your best at straight no-trick love.

But maybe straight no-trick love just doesn't work. My husband was screwing Audrey now, that coed tramp slut bitch, and people can call it fate all day long if they want because it is a free country and you can say what you like, but I called it damned stupid. When your husband is slipping away, you just can't sit back and let it happen. You've got to get smart fast and do something quick to stop it.

I could hear Miss New Jersey in the background somewhere saying, "For Christ's sake, Pamela, begin with getting your house back in order. Then, when you're through, go pick up Evie and leave the rat."

God, I hated to admit my mother was ever right.

I went and got the vacuum cleaner. In my contest gown, I sucked up every piece of dirt on every rug in my condo. Especially the dirt Audrey the tramp had tramped in. Then I put on my Playtex gloves and Windexed and Pine-Solled and Pledged all the surfaces of all the rooms, with my unzipped zipper touching my skin, cold with every stroke of the rag.

Then I began to throw everything away. Everything. Nothing was spared. Not even the little green recipe box so full of the notes Flick and Evie had left me over the years. Their little diary, there to remind me what a happy life we used to have.

I knew I'd regret throwing my box away. But the minute I had opened it hoping to find something to make me feel better, I just noticed more things to tear me up inside. The early years, our honeymoon years, were filed behind the "Appetizer" card: "I love you, Mrs. Outlaw, you gorgeous wife of mine. From your loving, handsome husband, Flick." The middle years, filed under the "Main Course: Meats and Casseroles" card, read: "I love you. Flick." And then there were the later middle-year notes filed under the "Muffin/ Biscuit" card: "Gone out for a bit. Love, me." And for the clincher, the last few years, filed under the "Dessert" card: "Be back soon, me." A menu from hell.

And if his little recipe for a sour marriage didn't upset my stomach, which it did, Evie's recipe for growing up practically killed me.

I mean, at what point had I become "Mom" to her? "Mom," with a hard Brooklyn o. And why had my sleaze bastard husband been able to remain "Daddy," still, to this day, when he was not even ever home to deserve it? I did not even know I had become "Mom." It did not even occur to me until that very minute, sitting at my kitchen table with Flick's notes scattered at my feet, when I noticed for the first time that her cute little notes of yesteryear where she spelled "Mommy" with an upside down y, had turned into the yummy dessert years of today where I had been pounded and floured and kneaded and stuck in the oven only to be pulled out and laid out on the baking rack as "Mom." No longer the sweet "Mommy" which had had such a comforting "me" sound attached to it—as if "Mom" and "me" were inseparable. But the hard lone sound of "Mom," singular. Somewhere along the way my little girl, my precious little Evie, had taken herself off and left me all alone. Just like her daddy had done.

After I furiously threw all those memories away, I packed a suitcase for me and one for Evie and then I put them in the trunk of my car. I had every intention of taking off and taking my little girl with me. I was not going to be me singular any longer. I was throwing those suitcases in the trunk, hard. I was lining up those diet drinks and Melba toasts and low-calorie snacks across the dashboard. I was ready to hit the highway, but then, dammit, a red Mercedes pulled up and Flick climbed out.

He walked up to me. He looked at me so sweetly. He put his strong arms of love around me and asked, "Pammy, are you okay?"

I broke down. "Oh, Flick, I am so, so sorry. I'm sorry about everything, anything, whatever I've done. I just want you back. I just want everything back to the way it was."

"I know, Pammy. I know. Me, too."

"I'll change, Flick. Just say what you want and I'll turn into it. Just say things will be back to the way they were." I was crying and holding him tight enough to break his ribs. "Just say you're still mine, Flick, and I'm still yours. The way you used to."

He kissed my face. He kissed little teeny kisses from my forehead to my chin and then he kissed them around to each ear. He kissed teeny little kisses on the top of my head. Then he kissed teeny tiny little kisses on my neck and you can just forget it when he gets there, because that is my crazy zone. He kept kissing me until he had kissed me back upstairs where we made long, quiet, special Pammy and Flick love all over our bed and I just knew everything was going to be okay.

Afterwards, we lay there and talked for a long time. Not about his affair, but about our first date. He had met me during a particularly rough time in my life. I'd just moved down south. I didn't have any friends. I'd just entered my first pageant and lost. Everyone circled me and made fun of my northern accent behind my back. I was an outsider. I knew when I lost that the proper etiquette was to stand on stage and smile, pretending the woman who did win Miss Lexington Five was, yes, the most perfect choice in the whole world, and that I should feel honored to simply stand beside her. So I did that little routine. I did what was expected of me. Then I tore home and cried for hours. Miss New Jersey kept knocking on my door trying to get me to come out. But all I wanted was to go back north where I belonged. I stayed in there for days. Then Flick Outlaw, this great looking guy who jogged around my neighborhood and talked to me every chance he got, showed up at my bedroom window and said, "Pammy, what's wrong? I don't ever see you out here anymore."

I, of course, did not answer. But one thing about Flick, he didn't take no answer for an answer. Instead, he said, "Okay. Come on. You're not staying in there any longer."

So. I went with him. Just like that. It was the first time I'd ever gone anywhere with a man without wearing makeup, without my hair sprayed into a perfect ball, without a show gown on and high heels. Instead, I was wearing tennis shoes, shorts and my beauty queen hair had turned into ratty hair from rolling around a wet pillowcase for days. He smiled at me and said, "You, Pammy Salowoski, are the most beautiful woman I have ever seen."

We got in his car and drove due north, straight out of town. I didn't have any idea where we were going, but I didn't care. I didn't speak. He rattled on about everything from physics, which I didn't know anything about, to what the best kind of barbecue was, which I certainly didn't know anything about. And I should have had some clue right in there as to how our lives were going to end up, but like I said, I just didn't care about anything except being in his car with him. About twenty miles out, he turned off at an exit and then he crossed over the overpass and turned back onto the highway, only this time he was heading due south. And he wasn't talking anymore. I guess I figured he was taking me back home. But after going a few miles down the same road we'd just come up, I saw it. I'd never been so thrilled. There it was in letters over a foot high, in red spray paint running all the way across the overpass:

FLICK LOVES PAMMY FLICK LOVES PAMMY
FLICK LOVES PAMMY FLICK LOVES PAMMY

I was so happy I squealed. And I squealed again when I saw it again on the next overpass. And on the next. And on the next. When we finally got back to town, I knew I'd never been so free and so pleased to be where I was and with who I was with. I knew if he wanted I would have gone to bed with him right there and then. But, of course, Flick had been too nice to take advantage of me which is probably why I ended up marrying him in the first place.

I snuggled close to him remembering that time. "Flick, remember our first ride down the highway? The overpasses? I loved that time so much."

"Yeah. It was fun, wasn't it?"

"God, it was everything, Flick. We should be like that again."

He didn't say anything. He was very still, but I could tell he was still awake.

"Flick?"

"Yes, Pammy?"

"Do you think we could do more of those things? You know, more of what we used to do when we were first together. To get it all back and keep it there."

Then he said, reaaaaal soft, "Sure, Pammy. Sure."

After he fell asleep, I slipped out of bed, quietly, so I wouldn't wake him up, got dressed, brushed my hair, cleaned out his wallet and walked right out of his stinking, cheating life.

7

How I planned to carry this off, to walk out of Flick's life and not tell my mother what was happening, was beyond me. The reason I didn't want to tell her was evident. We didn't get along. We disagreed on everything. We irritated the hell out of each other to the point of insanity. If you couldn't do the little things around each other, how could you talk about the big things? My mother could do the smallest, most insignificant thing, such as have a casual conversation over the phone with someone, and I could sit there and watch her play with a rubber band or a paper clip until suddenly Satan had jumped in my body and I was dreaming about grabbing the phone cord and wrapping it around her neck and hanging her from the ceiling fan. The paper clip or rubber band would fall to the floor and I'd be—I don't know—what? Miserable.

So why does it feel so good to think about ax murdering our mothers? And don't we all want to at least once during our lives? I'm beginning to think the abnormal person is the one who never felt that ax in their hand. I have pictured the back of my mother's beauty queen neck so many times, felt that cold hard ax handle squeezed tight in my palms, so many times, and for so many years I thought I must be a latent ax murderer and just didn't know it. It really used to bother me. I'd have bad dreams and wake up in cold sweats and hate myself. And then my little Evie comes along after so many years just to show me once again how normal it all was. And once again, she is probably wondering just how messed up she is.

Does she not know how many times I have felt her behind me, wanting to push me down the stairs? Does she think I don't know how many knives she's held with my heart in mind? Hasn't she dreamt night after night about slitting my throat and then the police are after her and suddenly she's on her way to jail where she'll never see her daddy again and she, too, wakes up in a cold sweat and feels depressed for the rest of the day because she is too young to know it is just a dream?

Yes, I know when my little girl has had those dreams, because she is there, right by my side for the rest of the day, wanting to help me wash the dishes, wash the fish tank, wash everything in sight so she can wash the dirtiness out of her evil little thirteen-year-old soul. It is days like that when I want to pick her up in my arms and say, "Oh, sweetie, don't do this to yourself. Don't you know that everyone feels just awful when they're turning thirteen? Don't you understand that as you get older, you'll still have days where you feel bad about yourself, but never as bad as when you're thirteen? Don't you know that your mommy knows you want to spill acid on her head while she sleeps? That's okay, honey, everyone wants to spill acid on their mommy's head while they sleep." But, of course, I can't tell her that.

The best I can do for her is to hug her up all day long for as long as she lets me, until I do something else that will make her want to break my neck.

I've finally grown up enough to know that it is normal to want to murder my mother some of the time, but I'm not so sure I will ever feel okay about wanting to strangle my own child. My child who ran out of Macayla Irvin's house wearing a black long-sleeved shirt because she hated her arms, long, black Lycra leggings because she hated her legs. The beautiful dress her grandmother had sent her was nowhere in sight. And worse, she didn't have any eyebrows. Well, she had eyebrows, but they were water soluble Maybelline eyebrows. Any other day I could have just said, forget it, Pammy. It'll pass. Turning thirteen is a hard time and if shaving her eyebrows helps her get through it, here is the razor. But this wasn't an ordinary day. I had just left a message on Miss New Jersey's phone machine telling her that Evie was primed and ready to win a northern pageant and we were on our way up. Just mention beauty contest to my mother and she doesn't have a lick of sense. All the questions like why wasn't Flick with me and was it okay for Evie to miss her last week of school would go flying out the window at the mere thought of one of her family members winning a crown under her direction.

But how was I going to explain Evie to my mother now? The last time she had seen Evie, at Christmas, she was still a sweet little twelve-year-old. I cannot push her into my mother's house and say, "We're here, Mom. Evie's brought her puberty with her." I cannot say that because my mother does not even know what puberty is. She did not let me have puberty. I tried to have puberty, but she just kept glossing it over just like her mother did to her and undoubtedly her grandmother did to her mother until we just jumped straight from being perfect little girls into perfectly screwed-up women. And then my little girl comes along after all these hundreds of puberty free years, and it is as if all the generations of puberties that have been kept down before are ready to come bursting forth out of her like water breaking loose from a dam. And day after day I'm turning into the Dutch boy who keeps poking one finger after the other into the dike. And now, when I don't have any choice but to go to my mother's, I find that I don't have any more fingers left to keep the water in.

Evie got in the car and slammed the door and I said, "Evie, don't slam the door."

And her puberty burst all over the place. "Don't call me 'Evie.' Call me 'Fern.' My new name is going to be Fern. Fern, always, get it?"

"Let me guess. You're Joan Crawford, right?"

She eyed me suspiciously. "How'd you know?"

"I guess I'm a damned genius, Fern."

She didn't speak so I didn't speak and we both just sat there thinking of different ways to kill each other and then she said, "Mrs. Irvin said she was the most popular movie star of all."

"Of course she would say that, sweetie."

Evie or Fern or Satan or whatever her name was shot me a hard dark look as we drove off into the Atlanta sunset. "Let me make a little educated guess, here," I said. "Macayla got to be Elizabeth Taylor, right?"

"No," she said snottily, looking at me as if she couldn't believe she'd been born to the stupidest mother on earth. "She was Brooke Shields."

"Oh, well. I was wrong by a fucking long shot, wasn't I?" I said, sarcastically.

"Mom, you don't have to cuss."

"Well, you're right, Fern. I am so fucking sorry."

"What is your problem anyway, Mom?"

And that was about the extent of our conversation as we drove away from the life that no longer was. Flick was no longer Flick. He was David. Evie was no longer Evie but Fern without any eyebrows. I was no longer nice, just fed up and sorry for myself and mad at everyone.

Just as I had watched the morning sun coming up, reflecting off the Capitol dome, now I was watching the evening sun go down over the dome, with the pigeons flying around in circles as I was driving out of town. Driving with Fern away from David to see Miss New Jersey.

These were the bad times.

These were the new times.

These were the times I had hoped I would never have to face.

But here I was.

8

The ride through Georgia was grim. It got dark. The roads were empty. I drove long stretches with the AM radio belting out hit tunes from Cuba so I wouldn't have to hear hit tunes from the United States that would send me running back to Flick. Little Miss Joan Crawford slept with her head in my lap, a sure sign that she had stayed up all night long the night before. Her eyebrows had smudged on my white slacks and she looked so much like her daddy. I wanted to pull over, pick her up in my arms and say, "I'm sorry we fought. I know it's because you're miserable about your mommy and daddy. It's okay if you want your mommy and daddy to stay together, because that's what Mommy wants, too." But I couldn't say that because for one thing, she didn't even know we had left him yet. I'd simply told her we were heading off for a little vacation at Nana's.

How would I finally tell her? I guess in the back of my

mind I knew it was in the back of her mind, but I didn't
think either one of us was ready to bring it up. Better to
keep it tucked safely away, until one day when she was
older, maybe in college and driving off to Daytona Beach
for spring break, she'd look out a car window and it would
vaguely remind her of another time when she was looking
out a car window. The time when her mother had packed up
all her clothes and took her off in the night away from the
one home she had ever really truly loved. Or maybe she
would remember lying on my lap, her mouth pressed
against my thigh, the radio playing a faraway static tango,
as I drove through South Carolina and stopped off in North
Carolina for gas. And how when we stopped, she had only
really truly woken up after her mommy had left the car to
pump gas. And she'd remember, mostly, how strange it had
felt to be awake at three o'clock on a school morning. And
she'd remember thinking that she felt good because of that,
but off center, too, like the birds that were singing and
chirping their day songs in the dark of the night. Neither she
nor the birds were supposed to be where they were, doing
what they were doing. But there they were, anyway, and
because of it, one day when she was twenty she'd remember
it and miss the smell of her mother, Pammy, me. She'd miss
the smell of me.

   And wasn't that the way I felt about my mother? Didn't I
miss being too young to care about anything in the world
but the way she smelled? And did my mother miss the way
her mother smelled, because she would never be able to
smell that smell again?

   Suddenly I was crossing over the Virginia state line,
thinking, God, I'm on the way to visit my mother and I
can't believe how happy I am! The first thing I will do is sit
on her bed and when she has gone into the kitchen to fix us

coffee I will open her drawers and take great big wonderful whiffs of her and be alive again!

Even if she hated me and I hated her and we would never agree on anything for as long as we lived, I knew that for as long as she lived, she'd always be there to take care of me if anything terrible happened. And that is more than I could say about anybody else. It was certainly more than I could say about Flick.

Ahhh! My great, wonderful mother who smelled like Estée Lauder Youth Dew; who ate all those diet delights such as tomato slices with cheese slices that tasted pretty much like pickles and leaves but somehow she managed to enjoy them. My mother, who had that nasty little rat terrier dog of hers who was deaf, blind and should have been put to sleep years ago, but who was still alive and trying to stand on three legs while he scratched his diseased skin off with his fourth. I couldn't even wait to see that stupid dog!

I couldn't wait to see my mother.

9

You know what gets me about that bitch? My mother, that's who. Okay. Fine. We walk in. Fine. She hugs us both. Fine. She sticks us in my old room, then serves us snacks. Fine. Fine. Fine. Everything is just fine. I've never been happier. Evie's never been happier. My mother's ecstatic. She's showboating around us. Giving us the grand tour of everything that has changed since our last visit. Well, nothing ever changes in my mother's house. But she shows us the little things. She wears her lacy summer gloves and points at the marbles in the lamp base; the cheesecloth on the back of the air conditioner to keep out the pollen; a new cedar pillow for Uncle Donald, her ratty rat terrier to sleep on. Normally I would have been stamping my foot for her to finish this dull trek through her dull life. But this time I'm thinking, "This isn't bad. This is not bad. I could be very contented draping cheesecloths on things. Forget Flick, forever. Just live here."

But then Evie says, "Nana, please call me 'Fern.' I'm not Evie anymore."

And she said, "Oh, what a marvelous name," and clapped her hands together.

"Mother, it isn't her real name."

"Oh, get over it," she said. Then she winked over my shoulder at Evie. "Like you didn't make everyone call you 'Tangerine.' "

The magic mother-daughter spell had been broken. Screw her cheesecloths and marbles. "I never made you call me that!"

"Certainly, you did. It was around the same time that stupid song came on the radio. What was that tragedy? Sure." She turned to Evie. "Some song called "Honey" where somebody dies and comes back again in their garden or as a horse or something, and Tangerine, here, would sit in her room and listen to that thing and wail. For hours she'd wail. I thought I was at the graveyard it was so spooky."

"Nana, did you really call Mom 'Tangerine'?"

"Of course I did. She just had to be Tangerine. I even entered her in one of the pageants as Tangerine Salowoski. And let me tell you, that's not a name that goes over so well with these Garden State judges."

I laughed, but I didn't think it was funny. "I never entered a contest under the name Tangerine, Mother."

"You didn't, huh? And I suppose you didn't get up there and read that stupid poem you wrote about Jesus and peace and let's all get together and be as happy as a bunch a little birdies, either. Fern, you wouldn't a believed it. There she is, standing in this white gauzy throwback she made me buy for her, and she's got flowers in her hair and she's up there and every word rhymes with the next. Me, be. Love, dove. Together, is better. Jesus, please us." Miss New Jersey was patting her heart, rocking back and forth, rolling her eyes, putting on a real show for Evie. "Christ! I thought I was going to have a heart attack watching all those judges laughing at her. But I got to tell you, it was funny."

We went into the kitchen where she poured Evie some chocolate milk. In my entire life she had never poured me a glass of chocolate milk. I was lucky to get skim milk. I was lucky I didn't get beriberi or rickets from the diet she had me on. "Well, I don't remember any of that, Mother. I think you're making it up," I said, smiling at Evie.

"I wish I were. But it's the God's honest truth," she said, raising her hand in the pledge of allegiance. "Lucky for me that judge's son had such an eye for you. You, the chameleon. Fern, if your mother had dated a convict, she would have worn stripes. You're looking at a woman who singlehandedly went through every personality in the dictionary. I'd given birth to Sybil I tell you."

Evie drank her milk in a second flat and pushed her glass at her grandmother for more. "Who's Sybil?"

"Sybil? I'll tell you who Sybil was. She was a woman who was a hag, a prostitute, a child, a nice lady, a man, even, I think. She'd turn into one thing and believe she was it until she turned into another thing."

Miss New Jersey hooked her head my way. "And your mother. You didn't know what was coming next with her. The child dated a talker, she became a talker. Yak, yak, yak, yak, yak. She dated a quiet boy, she became a quiet girl. She dated an idiot, she was a total idiot. She dated a Republican, oh, ah! To wake up and have Nixon-Agnew posters plastered all over the house! The worst kind of nightmare."

Miss New Jersey stopped for a minute and stared at her matching avocado-colored appliances. Then, softer, she said, "I didn't know where it was coming from. But then I figured, I just open my eyes and the next time that phone rings with a different boy on the other end of the line, she'd be metamorphosizing into something else, a Communist perhaps, behind her closed bedroom door. Always closed. Always locked. Always crying to some stupid song.''

"Mother!" I leaned against the stove with my arms crossed and tried to pretend like it was all so funny, but there are just some secrets you expect your mother to keep quiet about. Like the time you turned into a Republican.

"Then that Mike comes along. Fern, this was a boy who was seventeen, your mother's age, but he had this hair growing up his neck, down his back, running the length of his arms. He looked like he was forty-nine and had already been divorced twice.''

Mike, who slit tires, spit when he talked and was twenty-two but had a fake ID made just so he could date me, and I was madly in love with him.

Miss New Jersey raised her hands in the air. "That was when your grandaddy Joe moved us down south because of that pro-golf job. Some job, little Fern. It wasn't even at a country club. He told me it was a country club, but when we arrived there was no club. Only country. It was a driving range, I'm telling you, off the side of a highway. Count on my Joe to go to a state full of golf courses and end up with a job on a driving range. Go figure! So, there I am, contending with that, and Pammy brings home this Mike. You would have thrown up, Fern. I figured, okay, they make them older down south, or something, right? Hair growing up the front of his neck. Uck! He wasn't the kind of seventeen I wanted my daughter going out with. But what's a mother to do? Forty-nine, the guy looked, and my daughter's sneaking out with him.''

"Was he a creep?" Evie asked.

"Oh, he was much worse than a creep. He was a

slimeball. These were the days of the leisure suits and the
gorilla man comes flashing a new one by every day.''

Evie cracked up. ''Did they have double stitching?''

''Double stitching? Fern, these were the seventies. They
were triple stitched waffle patterned disasters. And he used
to come up to me and call me 'Mom' and hug me and I'd
slide right off that thing, I'm telling you. Aaaaack!''

Evie laughed and Miss New Jersey rolled her eyes.
''Then I find out he's Baptist and you could a struck me
dead. I didn't even know what a Baptist was. I mean, I
knew what one was, but I didn't know what one did.'' She
took a sip of Evie's chocolate milk and continued. ''That's
when I found out this was Tangerine's Jesus freak stage. I
tell you, she drove me crazy with all those phrases: 'God
loves you.' 'Jesus is Lord.' 'I found it.' 'We are His
children.' She painted them all over her walls and ceilings.
At one point she had it in her mind to do the entire Bible.
But she stopped at around the eleventh chapter in Genesis.
Anyway, I go to this church with her. Why do I go? I'll tell
you why. I go because she is my child and I love her, right?
Then I see why she's attracted to this church because they
all get together and hold hands and sing songs. Songs that
sound like that 'Honey' song. Yeah. The words rhyme and
you can cry to them if you want. I should a known she was
going to marry a Baptist. But I tell you. A mother can't
know everything.''

''Flick is a Methodist, Mother.''

''Methodist, Baptist. Same thing.''

I looked around her kitchen. Everything was spotless and
in its place. Had always been in its place. And was always
going to be in its place, because in her mind she was always
going to be Miss New Jersey 1950 something, and nothing
after the fifties existed for her. While everyone else rushed
through the sixties, seventies, eighties and nineties and

bought microwaves and Mr. Coffees, she held on to her old pop-up toaster and percolator. No copper pots hanging above her stove, thank you, but iron skillets which she had tenderly wiped with olive oil every day of her married life. While other people were now buying new wave waffle irons, french fry pots, blenders and popcorn makers, she still had the old ones which weren't new wave, but looked even more new wave than new wave because of the frantic need she had to polish everything in sight. I may have hated my mother, but I always loved her kitchen.

"Tell the story about Daddy, again," Evie asked, hugging her grandmother.

Miss New Jersey turned Evie around and began to play with her hair while she told the story of how I fell in love with Flick. "Well, I had your mother all set to marry this judge. Henry Gibson. I'll never forget him. He owned a heating–air conditioning company. Not bad, right? I'd never go cold, never get hot again." Nana blew in Evie's ear and Evie giggled. "And your mother. At first, she couldn't win a contest down south because of her northern accent. But then she gets smart and starts talking with a southern twang and she's winning all the contests. She's a beauty, too. All the judges want to date her. And she's dating all of them, believe you me. She thinks I don't know. She thinks I don't have eyes in the back of my head. But this Henry Gibson. Now he's different. He comes up to me and asks if he can date her. Asks me! Already I'm planning the wedding. This is the man who has respect. He knows how to show respect. And your mother wanted to marry. God forbid, every week she tells me she's going to marry this guy or that guy. She's driving me crazy with this marriage stuff. Other kids are getting subscriptions to *Seventeen* magazine, your mother's getting *Bride*, *Today's Bride*, *Modern Bride*, *Southern Bride*. So, it doesn't take a genius to see the girl wants to be a bride, right? So, I say, 'Okay Pammy. Just you make sure it's a judge.' Not because of the contests, little Fern, but you couldn't be a judge unless you owned your own business or had something going for you, right? None of the plaids and stripes of the homeless would show up on the doorstep of my daughter if she married a judge, I'm thinking."

Evie's head went back and back and back as her grandmother talked and stroked her hair. Her little neck was curved and smooth as a swan's. "Daddy wasn't a judge, but he worked."

Miss New Jersey scrunched her mouth and rolled her eyes at me. "Let me tell the story, little Fern. So, she and I agree on her marrying one of the judges. We never agree on anything but this much. So, she meets this Henry and falls in love with him. I'm thinking, the gods are with me, right? What more could you want than for your daughter to marry well? A good provider is a good man. Yeah. But then something terrible happens. Henry Gibson falls right back in love with her. And, ohhh, the minute he falls in love with her, in her great Pammy Salowoski style, she takes off and marries your father behind my back. 'Why,' I ask her? Knowing full well that the answer is she just doesn't want anyone to be in love with her. Oh, and you could take one look at Flick and see that he's Mr. Slick. He doesn't just stand, he poses. He doesn't only know all the answers, he knows all the questions. He's so perfect that he's perfectly wrong, is what I'm thinking. She's going to have to do all the work, is what I'm thinking. But maybe that's what she wants, is to do all the work. Who can tell? Some women just don't want love to come easy. Well, I ask why. 'Why Mr. Slick?' And do you know what she says? She says, 'Because he's handsome.' "

Evie turned around and hugged Miss New Jersey again and I smiled because I did remember that part. Flick and his

perfect mouth and that beautiful blond hair of his that Evie
would get. His green eyes and his big hands and neat laugh,
all fitting together, coming together to make me love him so
much. I remember standing there, telling my mother all
about him. And she forbid the entire affair. When I had
asked her why, she said, "Pammy, there's something wrong
with a man who's got nothing wrong with him."

I guess I never really knew what she meant until now.

"I ask you," she said, tickling Evie. "What kind of
answer is that to say your father's handsome?"

Evie laughed. "He is handsome."

"Handsome shmandsome. Marry a rich man and get him
a facelift, is what I would have told her today, but men
didn't get facelifts back then. So. I was in a bind." She
began massaging the back of Evie's neck while she talked,
going off into the past, remembering where it all fell apart
for her, total loss of control over the one thing she'd always
had control over—her daughter.

"That Henry Gibson would show up. Your mother wouldn't
come down. We'd sit on the sofa for hours talking, waiting
for her. And okay, so he turns out to be a bore. But he was a
sweet bore. But still, he was there. Night after night.
Faithful like a dog. Meanwhile, your mother's setting up
dates with Mr. Slick on the same nights. Only, Mr. Slick
doesn't show half the time. So your mother locks herself in
the bedroom and wails while your dear sweet grandmother,
me, is entertaining Henry. Night after night after long night.
I'm thinking, okay, so he's truly, truly boring. But at least
he is not the reason my little girl is upstairs wailing like a
drowning woman."

"Tell me how boring he was," Evie asked. She loved this
part, of course. She just cracked up every time her grandmother told it to her.

Miss New Jersey squeezed her hard, then continued.

"Aggressively boring. So, anyway, one time Henry sets this thing up with his mother. Ayyy! I'm going to be stuck on the sofa with him and his mother now. I told your mother, Tangerine here, if you don't come, I'm going to cut you out of my will. So, she swears she'll be there, right? I mean, this sweet woman must of spent hours dressing to meet my girl. So. There I am with Henry and his mother, Lucy. That was her name. Lucy. We're all sitting on the sofa with nothing to do but wait for Pammy to come down the stairs."

The coffee began to percolate. The sound made me homesick for my mother, even though I was right there with her. The kitchen smelled the way it had when I was a child. I just wanted to take that sound, that smell, wrap them up into my arms and hold them that way forever. And somehow, that smell, that sound and my mother holding my daughter all came together so peacefully. I may have hated my mother for telling my daughter that I was ever a Republican, but I knew I'd come to the right place.

My mother can be such a beast sometimes. But other times she can surprise me. When I'm in the crunch she surprises me. Once I had a strange little accident when I was about Evie's age. I was sliding down the banister and I clipped my nipple halfway off at the end of the run. Of course, I did not want anyone to know. I was just sprouting breasts! And that was the point. Somewhere down the line I must have read that if you hurt your breast, you'd get breast cancer, which was a lie. But I was at that age where all lies, especially the evil dark scary ones, were so true. So. I was too afraid to tell my mother about it, much the same way I felt now about bringing my problem with Flick out in the open.

I probably needed stitches when I hurt my breast, but I secretly patched it up with Band Aids and wouldn't come out of my room to go to school the next day. My mother kept asking, "But why, Pammy? You don't have a fever. Where does it hurt?" Still, I wouldn't speak to her. Eventually, she just gave up and stayed home from bridge and rubbed my forehead with a peppermint scented washcloth and she sang the songs to me she used to sing when we were traveling to fun places: "Johnny with the Bandied Leg," "Down in the Meadow in the Itty Bitty Pool," "Try to Remember." God, I felt so protected then. She never asked what was wrong. Of course, I seem to remember that it wasn't long after that, probably the very next day, when I found a giant box of Kotex looming large on my bed when I returned home from school. God, that was embarrassing. But still, she never asked what was wrong, I never told her, but she managed to keep me safe from it anyway.

I had that same feeling of being protected now. Those times before I was a fully developed Pammy were here again. I was that little girl all over again. I didn't want to tell my mother the problem, but I also wanted her to take care of it. And when the scare was over, I'd go outside and play, a normal girl, having a normal life.

"And the next thing I know," my mother says to my daughter, "is Pammy got married. My little Pammy eloped. Your grandaddy Joe quit his job at the so-called country club and we moved back north. Oh, it was awful. I had to leave my baby girl down there with all those Baptists."

Miss New Jersey's little rat terrier got up from his spot on the floor and circled like a drunk around the table. Then he returned to his new cedar bed and went back to sleep. Evie looked up at her grandmother, her grandmother looked down at her. "But then she had you, my precious little Fern, and there was a happy ending after all, wasn't there?"

10

How would she know? How in the hell would Miss New Jersey know anything? She wouldn't know a happy ending if it came up to her in the frozen food section of the Piggly Wiggly and bit her on the ass. Hell, if her relationship with her husband was half as good as mine is with Flick right now, that would be the closest she'd have ever come to a happy ending. The classic scenario of my mother and her husband, Joe, goes as follows: He walks into her kitchen. Immediately they are two cats with their back hairs shot up. Joe looks at Evie, who has not finished her second glass of chocolate milk, and screams at her, because when he talks he screams, "Why didn't you finish your milk? Drink it. It'll put hair on your chest."

Miss New Jersey smiles warmly at Evie, but responds coldly to him, "Maybe she doesn't want any hair on her chest, Joe. Leave her alone."

"But it'll put hair on her chest, Lillian," he yells again,

as if we have not already heard him once. "When I was a boy, I ate everything my parents ever put in front of me. I wouldn't leave the table until I was finished. There are people starving in the world, you know. You can't let good food go to waste. That's the trouble with you young people. You don't care about anybody." Then he tacks on, "Eh? Eh?" He always tacks on the eh? eh?

But just as one dog can't let the other have the last bark, neither could my mother ever let Joe. This time it was, "Shut up, already. Go hit some balls. Get out of here. Nobody wants to hear you pontificating already, all right?"

God, I used to think he hated me so much. And now my little girl comes along after all these years to show me just how much it was Miss New Jersey who he hated. He hadn't been attacking me. And he hadn't been attacking Evie, either. Well, maybe he had. But what I think was that he didn't see us as people. He saw us as the property of Miss New Jersey, the unattackable. If he couldn't get to her directly, he'd try to get to her through us.

As if that had ever worked.

Joe yelled at Evie, "I was in the army for fourteen years and we ate everything on our plates. Sure, they only had men in the army then. But they got some women in now. Everybody should join the army for two years. It builds character. No reason why a girl like you can't join. Eh? Eh?"

Poor little Evie. I wanted to take her in my arms and squeeze her and say, "Oh, honey, it's okay if you want to tell Grandaddy Joe to go to hell. Everybody wants to tell Grandaddy Joe to go to hell." But, of course, I couldn't tell her that. The best I could do was stare at him and wonder what my mother saw in him. They were a pair. A woman who lived off an inheritance that I would never see because she was married to a slob with no job and one of the most expensive habits in the world—golf—second only to crack cocaine.

Miss New Jersey chased Joe out of the kitchen and into his workroom where he would spend the rest of the day cleaning his nine hundred golf clubs and fifty pairs of golf shoes, sulking until the old Jackie Gleason reruns came on. Then they'd be back together again, side by side in their matching La-Z-Boys where, for one solid half hour, they'd be in love. And then the minute the half hour was up, the hair would be back on the chest, Joe would be trudging the nine miles in the snow to get to school every morning, while campaigning for everyone to join the army and grow hair on their chest.

The only time this ever varied was when a golf tournament came on television. Then everybody had a five hour reprieve from Grandaddy Joe, and he and Miss New Jersey would bond together, man and wife, La-Z-Boy to La-Z-Boy, while the golf commentator did the only whispering that had ever been heard in their marriage. And my mother questioned my happy ending? Give me a break.

Well, there was no golf match on this day and Jackie Gleason didn't come on until night, so Miss New Jersey chased him out of the kitchen and Evie and I heard horrible screaming. Just horrible. It ended with him finally shouting, "What do you want? You want me to get the hell out and stay out? Speak up, lady. Eh? Eh?"

Silence. Then we heard him say, "Ah, forget it, Lillian. I'm going to go hit a bucket a balls."

I put my finger to my lips and motioned for Evie to remain quiet. Then Miss New Jersey walked in smiling and rubbed Evie behind her ears. "Don't pay any attention to us, dear. It's just a lovers' spat. Why don't you go out there and hit a few golf balls with your grandaddy Joe? He thinks you don't love him."

"Okay, Nana," Evie said, jumping up and kissing her on the cheek, ignoring me completely. As if it didn't hurt. I mean, doesn't she know I'd like a nice kiss now and then? Doesn't anybody ever look at me and think, "Pammy could use some attention?"

Apparently not. Because not long after Evie followed Joe, Miss New Jersey climbed into her big bronze Cadillac and headed out for the day. And I guess I could have ended my story here, with me back where I had started, with my mother going off to have her hair done, and me sitting on the edge of my bed hoping she wouldn't ever come back.

But I cannot leave well enough alone to end anything. I mean, I couldn't even end my marriage with Flick. It is easy for a woman to see a hotel receipt which attaches her husband to another woman, then leave him the next day. It is easy when she leaves to think she is finished with him for good. But what is not easy, and what breaks down the big resolve to leave, is finally being left alone after the great rush to leave is over.

The minute my mother walked out of her house, I turned into a total weenie. I called Flick. I knew I shouldn't be so stupid. I tried not to be. I circled the damn phone like a snake for five minutes trying to talk myself out of it.

But a woman in love can always find some tiny table scrap of reason to call a man when she's being served a big plate of logic that says she shouldn't call him. My one little scrap was: who was going to feed my fish? After all, I was a mother. I wanted things to grow and thrive and live. The thought of Beatrice and Sam and Gertrude and Gretel spiraling down to their watery graves at the bottom of the toilet was almost more than I could bear. So, there was no question that I would call Flick.

I picked up my mother's princess phone, baby blue with a rotary dial, and let the line from New Jersey to Georgia ring and ring and ring. Nobody answered. Then somebody answered. In fact, a squat graduate student with a smooshed-in face named Audrey the coed tramp slut bitch. "Outlaw residence," she said.

I said, "Oh, hey, Audrey!" Like she was my best friend and I was so happy to hear her stinking cheating slutty voice. "Is Flick there?"

"No, Pammy," she said, "He's not." As if I had disturbed her.

Then the little tramp said nothing else. She just waited for me to talk, to work for any information I needed. But all I could say was, "Okay, well, then, talk to you later, bye-bye," in this singsongy voice that I will never ever, for the rest of my life, no matter how long I live, ever forgive myself for having used. I mean, other, more normal women would have said, "Audrey, why don't you go jump off the face of the earth," but I wasn't normal. I was just Pammy Outlaw, who didn't want to make waves and lose my husband. Who didn't want to do something the way my mother would have done.

But why not? What was wrong with being my mother once in a while? I mean, at least my mother still had her husband. He may not have been much, but he was around. So I picked up the phone and dialed again, so angry I was screaming. And damn those stupid rotary dialers! You just can't dial them fast enough. And if you try your fingers slip out of the holes and before you know it you are standing there with your body shaking and you are shaking your fist in the air and you are ready to fight. Only the tramp in Georgia you want to fight with has already walked out of your house and is starting up her car to go find your husband so she can make trampy love with him all over Atlanta and you are left with a stupid breaking heart and nothing to fight with but a damn rotary phone.

I threw it on the floor, screaming at it, and watched it not break. And then, I began to laugh. It was just like the unbreakable Miss New Jersey to surround herself with unbreakable objects. Maybe that's why I couldn't talk to her about Flick. Somehow I couldn't imagine how she'd deal with a daughter who was breaking right in two.

11

Oh, I missed Flick's voice so much it was unbelievable. Unbearable. If I could have just heard him say my name one more time. He had this really nice way of saying "Pammy" where he held a couple of beats on the end, making it sound as if my name ended in four *e*'s instead of a *y*. Pammeeee. But now it seemed as if all I ever heard anymore was the voice of Miss New Jersey yelling through the bedroom door, "Pamela!"

"What, mother?" I asked, not opening it.

"My usual little Friday night crowd's coming over. I want you to dress up and come out of your room. They'll be bringing a few more people with them to meet my grownup little Fern."

I looked at the clock. It was already Friday night. I had slept the whole day, I had slept for fifteen hours straight. The first thing I thought about was what Flick had done while I had slept; what he had done or thought since I'd last seen him some thirty-odd hours ago. I couldn't shake the terrible feeling inside me. It was as if I were just a ghost of myself. My real true self had pulled out and away from me, abandoning me, too. I felt lighter, my blood felt thinner, my upper arms felt weird. If someone had come along and picked me up, I would probably have kept on going, up and up and up, as if I weighed only eight ounces. Without Flick, there was nothing left of me.

Well, I didn't want the Friday night crowd to come but the Friday night crowd came anyway. Lou and Uncle Sam and Annie and Donna. And they brought some friends, who in turn brought some friends, who in turn brought one of my stupid ex-boyfriends, and before I knew it I was swirling around the room drunk not even noticing that Evie was getting drunk, too. The only thing I was noticing was that Uncle Sam, who really wasn't my uncle, but an old friend of my mother's, wasn't so old anymore. He was sweet and sexy and, well, just very, very sexy and all I could think about was how rotten I was to be missing my husband so badly while I so badly wanted to run my fingers up and down Uncle Sam's chest. And how, in thinking that one of my mother's friends was sexy, I had crossed over the line and was zipping towards middle age.

I'd already kissed my ex-boyfriend. I'd pulled him out the door and into Joe's workroom and went right to it, pretending he was Flick, but that didn't work. I didn't get excited. So I pretended he was Uncle Sam, and that did it. But you know drunks. They have their mind set to do one thing and then they are doing another. I'd had my mind set on committing adultery all over Grandaddy Joe's pool table to get Flick back for committing adultery on me, but then, for some reason I began laughing and then throwing up and then I was back upstairs drinking some more and then Evie was throwing up. And then I was crying.

I was a horrible wife. I could not keep my husband. I was
a horrible mother. I could not keep my daughter from
drinking. And there wasn't anybody I could talk to about
any of it. I put Evie to bed and rubbed her forehead with a
wet washcloth and fell asleep beside her. I fell asleep
thinking I should kill myself. That's how bad I felt.

But then, I'm not really sure what happened next except
that I was in Uncle Sam's Peugeot, asleep and drooling on
his pants leg, and the sun was coming up and he was pulling
into a small airport and I don't know. I guess it was the way
the sun was gleaming off the wing of this one single-engine
plane, parked next to all these twin engines which hadn't
been lighted by the sun at all; something about the sun
choosing the smallest plane made me feel good again. I was
small and insignificant, too. Maybe the sun would shine on
me.

"Where are we?" I asked Uncle Sam, rising, stretching
and suddenly remembering that I had furiously tried to make
out with him all night long. Grabbing him where I shouldn't
have, and grabbing and grabbing and grabbing him until I
thought I was going to go insane with desire. And him, just
saying no, no, no, and me just laughing and laughing and
saying oh but yes, yes, yes. And now I had to face him.
And I was no longer drunk. Ooooo.

"We're at the Morristown Airport. I think I've got a great
way to raise your spirits."

He ordered me a breakfast I would never be able to eat in
a hundred years while he went to chart out his flight plan. It
was a busy little airport. It seemed as though every time a
plane landed something else came back to me. I stared at
my eggs and remembered blowing in Uncle Sam's ear and
then crying all over the dashboard as I told him the complete
Flick and Pammy tragedy. The entire Pammy and Flick love
story. Then, horror of horrors, I told him I'd never really

loved anybody as much as I had loved him, Uncle Sam,
who, frankly, up until that night hadn't been much more
than a man who used to come by when I was a little girl to
play golf with my stepfather and bring me packs of Juicy
Fruit gum. I even told him about my Barbie dolls and how I
used to dream that he was Ken. Which wasn't true, but
when I was drunk it seemed like a clever thing to say.

He came back, pulling a chair over from the other table,
and watched me watch the runway. He said, "Are you
feeling better?"

I looked up at him, feeling pretty sheepish. "Yes. Well,
no. Does my mother know where I am?"

"Yes. I told her I had a job and I needed some help and
that you had volunteered. She was thrilled."

"Did she buy it?"

"Frankly, I don't think she gave it a second thought. She
seemed excited about having a day alone with her granddaughter. Your mother really loves that little girl of yours."

"Thank you." I watched the small plane taxi down the
runway. "Did everyone know I was drunk?"

"Probably just Flick."

"Flick!"

"Well, do you remember that he called you?"

"No!" I was horrified. My heart dropped.

"At first you wouldn't talk to him. But then you called
him back."

"Oh, my God! I don't remember this!"

"No," Sam said. "You were great. You told him exactly
what you needed to. You were flat, unemotional, diplo-
matic, nice. He'd be an idiot not to want you back now. You
were incredible."

"I was? This doesn't sound like me. I'm not an incredible
woman."

"Pammy," he said, and he took my hands. "You probably don't remember, but we talked about it for a long time before you called him back. And I told you how to do it, the way a lawyer would do it, and that's exactly what you did."

"Oh, my God! Did my mother hear? I didn't want my mother to know about this."

He laughed. "I'm telling you. She's too involved with preparing her little granddaughter for all the pageants in the world to know what's going on around her. Besides, you called him from my house." Then he winked and added. "On my lap."

I died. "Oh my God. I'm so embarrassed. All I remember is the car."

That's when he leaned across the table and kissed me. And I can't quite explain how, but it was the sweetest kiss I've ever known. It was as if in kissing me, he put the real me, the true Pammy, back inside where only the ghost had been. I sat back, blushing, as I watched the small plane take off and I felt as if I were taking off with it.

12

God, I'm turning into a little girl again, even down to the fantasies I'm having. How can this happen? This great transformation from a woman who knows to shift her eyes away from a flirting man in the grocery store because she is married, to a woman who no longer has a reason to look away?

There I was, kissing Sam, and it was wonderful. Only I kept getting this feeling that I was doing something really horrible. Which I wasn't. And I kept getting this feeling that Flick was going to show up any minute and catch me. Which he wasn't. In the first place, if he did come after me, the last place he'd come would be Jockey Hollow National Park on a side road behind some of George Washington's old soldiers' huts.

In the second place, he wasn't going to come, period. That's why kissing Sam was not so horrible. Flick had released me from all the obligations of something I had never intended to be released from—our marriage. And okay, maybe it was never really all that good between us. Maybe with Flick I never truly felt comfortable. Maybe there was an emptiness, a real loneliness that hovered over our marriage, our love, our sex, but I tell you, that is not the point. The point is, just because another man came along after all these years to touch me in a way Flick never could, I still couldn't help but think about Flick. In its stilted stiff uncomfortable way, Flick's love was in my blood. So when Sam touched me in such a way as I never believed could be true it made me think about hell, for surely if I felt that good with a man other than my husband, wasn't there a bright sunny spot for me in that love-crime fire?

God, I was only kissing him, but I tell you, a man that tall and that warm and that sexual presses up against the cold and lonely body of a woman who has been rejected and can't accept it yet, well, the sin of it all makes the pleasure of it all even that much greater. All I could think about was pulling my dress up, turning his sheets back and Flick, walking in on us and really leaving me forever.

Well, I'd already been left. Couldn't I fantasize without him rejecting me again? Couldn't I even have fun thinking about it? Other more normal women might have the husband walk in on a hot sexual dream and have him fall to his knees in shame and forgiveness. But I couldn't be a normal woman with Flick. He wasn't that cut and dried. I might have thought he was through with me, the way he'd been acting you'd almost swear he was finished, but you can never be sure with a man like my husband.

How do I know? I'll tell you how I know. I don't. I just know he's a real strange one when it comes to love. Like when he spray painted his love for me on the overpasses. I thought for sure I was falling for a guy with, you know, a flair for the theatrical. But that was all there was—that one little burst. And then. Nothing. When we got married I wasn't so sure Flick was even in love with me. I just figured he must have been to want to marry me. But I tell you, he would not hold my hand in public, he would not give me eye contact in front of other people, he would not even introduce me half the time. So I was like, okay, buddy, this isn't working. Let's call this thing off and he goes and asks me to marry him anyway? With those signals to run on, how could I ever be sure that he never wanted to see me again now? How could I be sure I wasn't just reading him wrong? With a man like Flick, you had to pretty much go on nothing, because all the instinct, all the reasoning, all the anything you could count on with other men went right out the window if you tried to apply it to him. He had this inner kind of darkness that pulled him along, that made him go into our bedroom and close himself off from the rest of the world, that made him hug me when I least expected it and never hug me when I needed it most. The most you can do with a man like that is close your eyes, cross your fingers and don't count on anything and don't count anything out.

I used to find that so sexy. I used to think whatever it was that made my husband tick was this special mystery and I was the only woman in the world who would ever be able to reveal the wonderful secrets that were in there.

It was only later, maybe in the last two years, when I began to unravel that mystery and see it for what it was—a severe depression that had him locked up, lock, stock and barrel. God, and to think I used to believe I had rubbed up against some kind of specialness.

Well, I tell you. When you wake up one morning and brew coffee and look at the back of your husband's neck and finally see him for what he really is, that doesn't mean you love him less. It probably just means you will take those little sicknesses within yourself and match them up to his.

Some great flashing stupidness will take over leading you to believe that this is what marital bonding is all about. Suddenly it is like, oh, so what, you're crazy and I'm crazy but we are in this thing together.

One of the few things Sam said to me while I was drunk was this. I was crying all over his car, his shirt, the ground, wailing and screaming that I must be crazy to be so stupid. I must be crazy to be such an idiot. I must be crazy if I was always feeling this way. "Sam, I can be standing in the bright sunlight watching my little girl play and half the time I feel as if I'm in a small dark closet and someone's holding a pillow over my face so I can't breathe. I can't explain it."

He said, "Pammy, don't you know everyone feels that way most of the time?"

"They do?" I had said, drying my eyes.

"Of course they do. Everybody thinks if you just pulled a little thread, it would all come loose."

I thought about my little thread. It seemed as if it had already been pulled and pulled until there wasn't any more thread left to be pulled and the worst that had happened was that I felt pretty lousy. That made me feel better. That made me want to have Sam. Because I'm telling you, when a man comes along and takes your biggest fear; the fear that you're going mad, and casually tosses it out the car window, you want to have sex with him.

So there I was, back to Sam, which brought me back to Flick. It was as if I were standing in the middle of a football field holding a football in each hand, and everybody was charging after me. One football was Flick. One was Sam. The charging people were my hormones, I'm sure, because I can never seem to leave my hormones out of anything.

The funny thing about Sam was this. Even the next day when I wasn't drunk and I saw that this was a man I could be in love with, I wasn't in love with him. I wasn't even infatuated with him. I just wanted to kiss him. And I wanted to go to bed with him. And I probably never wanted to come out of that bed. And I wanted to listen to him talk to me forever because nobody had ever said so many wonderful things to me in my entire life. And I wanted to touch his hands, his face, his neck, squeeze his arms, put my pinky in his mouth and stare in his eyes. But even adding all of that into the pot, I'd have to say, I was still in love with the one man who had never made me feel any of those things. And just thinking about all of that made me feel crazy again. That little string was back at the base of my brain and somebody was about to pull it as if I were a Chatty Kathy doll, only instead of chatting, I'd be shattering—the pieces on the ground simply fragments of what once used to be a sane woman.

When I told Sam this, because somehow I could tell Sam anything, he said, "Pammy, the only rule I've ever found that applies to love is that there is no rule. It doesn't have to make sense. If it makes any sense at all, it probably isn't love." And what's even better than that, he grabbed his heart and said, "Did I say that? If I ever start talking that way again, shoot me."

I spent my first week in New Jersey that way, with Sam talking to me while I kissed him. I let my mother take care of Evie, as if I had a choice. I even left it up to her to talk to Evie about getting drunk. And although it was slack on my part and I don't really know what she told her, I knew she would hawk over her the same way she had hawked over me and I never turned into an alcoholic.

Another wonderful thing about Miss New Jersey was that she never asked me about Flick. I never told her either. I just blurred everything over with some feeble excuse about how he needed to be alone to study for his comps. I didn't even really know what a comp was. Miss New Jersey didn't care. She never asked me about Sam either, but I kept decent hours with him so Evie wouldn't think I was up to something. And I wasn't. Sam and I weren't doing a thing other than having a more romantic time than I'd ever had in my life.

Flick would call. It's not like he was a complete jerk. He made his calls to me just like he made his sales calls—right around a quarter to five when people were rushing to close up shop so they could get home. Flick figured it was the best time to get quick information out of people fast. And it worked. I'm just not so sure it worked with me. For one thing, I didn't know what kind of information he wanted. The ball was pretty much in his court; it's just that one side of his court was in Atlanta named Audrey the slut tramp bitch troublemaker, while the other side was in New Jersey with his child, thinking about total custody. And I *was* thinking about it. I will not lie. I just wasn't going to tell him about it. Not yet anyway, because Sam had said, "Pammy, you probably don't want to bring that up until you have some idea of where you stand with him. Also, there's a chance you don't really mean it. There's a chance you're just mad."

"No, I mean it," I had said. But he was probably right. I was pissed. Mostly, I think, at myself. I mean, where was I during all that adulterating time? I still can't quite get it. It was as if Flick and I were a picture perfect couple, but then someone casually comes along and turns the picture over and I find out that we weren't a picture at all, but a puzzle, and now all the pieces were on the floor. Only this affair hadn't happened that casually. No. This Audrey thing took days, weeks, months to plot and plan and heat up and work itself into my life. And I did not even see it coming. Why? Because, well, I don't know why. I guess I was busy doing things. But what things?

Oh, God! Here's one. I was busy trying to get one of the

four college boys in the town house next to us to date the slut tramp bitch. I couldn't help it. I felt so sorry for her. She'd come over on Friday and Saturday nights and I'd make dinner and look at her pitiful face and think, who is going to date this poor creature? So I shifted into gear trying to find someone, never even guessing that she'd already found someone for herself.

And she was witty. It's not like she wasn't witty. So I'd remind Flick of all the witty things she said so maybe he'd be on the lookout for some of his graduate friends who might like a witty girl. Oh, I'd just go on and on about all of her brilliant qualities, trying to sell her to my salesman husband who had unfortunately already been sold.

And I guess a lot of my time had been spent with Evie's beauty queen pageants, although for the life of me, I can't see why that was ever so important to me. Looking back on it all, Flick and me and how we aren't going to make it, and Sam and how he is so big in my life so fast, I wonder how I could have ever enjoyed a walk down a beauty pageant runway. I'm wondering how I could ever have put my little girl through such a thing.

That's one of the things Flick said when he made one of his 4:45 calls on the dot. "Pammy, I just don't understand why you do that to Evie?"

And now I say, "I know. Me neither." Although I know it won't matter what I say now. Because I hear in his voice that he has already given up on me. I hear him trying not to give up, but it's as if he's already walked out the door and what I'm listening to is the echo of what he has said.

But it's so maddening, this not knowing, because, like I said, with Flick, you can never know.

13

Seven, eight, nine days of separation from Flick are crossed off the calendar, spring turns into summer, rain turns into sun and there I am, turning into Sam's. It was not an easy transformation. It was usually, one day I was sad about Flick, the next day I was ecstatic about Sam, the next day more sadness about Flick, then suddenly I'd feel happy to be away from him again.

No more picking his hairs out of the sink. No more soaking out his hardened cereal bowls. No more grabbing the socks he'd washed in his bathwater off the towel rack. And no more reading those horrible books.

I still remember the first book Flick gave me to read. Before the book of poems. This time it was a book which had long footnotes on every page, sometimes longer than the text itself. And it was a thin book—sixty-five pages—and it cost about a dollar a page. It wasn't long after I read it that I realized it had probably cost me my marriage.

Flick had said, "Pammy, will you do me a favor and read this?"

I innocently took that book from him and sat down to read it. That was in the morning. By evening, I was still reading. But do you think I could actually follow that crap? Hell, I couldn't believe people actually wrote it! And I had to rewrite it just so I could understand it.

Just one of the sentences, diagrammed, resembled the molecular structure of saturated fat. Something I myself had seen a million times in diet books. And the stupid thing was, once broken down, those sentences said nothing. Zilch! Long sentences of forty-five words saying what the normal housewife could have said in ten.

The first third of the book, broken down, simply said that when we read, we bring our own thoughts to the page. Brilliant observation. The next third, rewritten, said that without a reader a book is not read. Major breakthrough. I'm wondering what's the sixty-five-dollar point here, right? Then I get to the last chapter, which promises me this great buildup in the conclusion, and I turn the page and the whole damn thing is written in French!

Well, I am sorrrrrry, but I don't read French. I do not even think I know anyone who does. I mean, did Flick read French? And if he did, when did he learn it? And why, knowing I didn't, had he given me something like that to read?

I said, "Flick, you've got to be kidding, right?"

He said, "What do you mean?"

"What do you mean, what do I mean?" I said. "I mean, I don't read French. Why did you give me French to read? Did that writer think everyone knew how to read French? Is this a trick?" I have to admit, I was pretty mad.

Flick kind of laughed. I thought he was laughing at me so then, of course, I got madder. "Look, Pammy. Most critical theorists write for the college professor and most college professors read French, so a lot of these writers assume the average critical theory reader will understand. I'm sorry. I forgot."

"You forgot what? That it ended in French? Or it slipped your mind I didn't know any? And by the way, do you?"

It was then that I realized Flick had been learning French all along. And it was at that precise moment when I knew nothing would ever be the same for us again. I stood in our blue checkered South Carolina kitchen, holding that book out to him, listening to him and then not listening to him, but wondering if he would ever get around to changing the overhead light before he left me. One bulb had burned out weeks ago and two had followed, leaving us forty lousy watts to work our crummy little lives out in.

Some more intelligent woman might stop me on the street and say, "Pammy, didn't you know your husband was sick of sales? I mean, sweetie, you poor pitiful idiot, didn't it even occur to you that he had ambitions of becoming a Ph.D.? Are you really so dumb you didn't see an affair coming on?" No, I'd say. It's not that I'm dumb. I saw the strained looks in the morning when he had to go out and face clients he couldn't stand. I'd watched him going in later and later and coming home earlier and earlier. I'd noticed him shuddering every time the phone rang. The signals were all there and I would have been a fool not to see something coming. But the thing is, you get to where you get used to things and when changes do come, you take in what you're ready for. You see things, and either you are smart enough to see them for what they are, or you are just chicken enough to turn them into what you want to see them as. And I was never one to see something for what it was. My philosophy remained pitiful throughout my marriage:

turn my back on things I didn't want to know, bury my head in the sand and eventually they would go away.

And I'm not so sure that's a bad thing to do. You have to do some of that in a marriage or the marriage isn't going to work out. You see those socks in the bathtub, those half-empty cereal bowls crammed in a bookcase somewhere, those hairs on the bathroom soaps and you say to yourself, "This is the way things are. Get used to it."

Then you see your husband looking pinched and you think, "This is the way things are, too."

I guess that explained my shock when Flick casually announced one morning that he wasn't going to work anymore. He was going to finish his master's, get a Ph.D. and go on to become a professor at a university. I just sat there and stirred my coffee and thought, "Finish his master's? When had he even started one?"

It was then that I realized he'd had these ambitions all along. It was then when I began to get scared. I hadn't even bothered to care about his past or future. I'd just figured after he married me, the Watermelon Queen, what else could be out there for him? I was the perfect wife. The perfect mother. I was beautiful.

I guess I kind of smiled or something, as he explained how this little educational jaunt would only take four or five years out of our lives; how we wouldn't be broke because he had been saving for this all along; how he planned to go ahead and do something I never dreamed he ever wanted to do which would eventually ruin our lives together.

I mean, at least he wasn't talking about leaving me. At least he wasn't talking about a girlfriend.

So instead of yelling, I said, "Flick, if you want to go to school, you just go on and go to school. You know you can always count on me to stand by your side."

And all that time I was standing by his side and he was

taking his side away from me so I couldn't stand by it. All that time I had kept telling myself, "So what if he needs a change. A man going bald might need a little change. He's vulnerable. He probably thinks he is dying and he is trying to grab hold of life. But he will certainly stay with the beauty queen, because in me, he can see that he is still a virile and strong man."

Well, if I had to do it all over again, I would just have to shake my head and say, "No, Pammy. You don't want to do this. You do what you have to do, but whatever it is, do not let him make this move. Let whatever it is pass. Because eventually it will pass. Before it passes, he may bitch and moan and make you feel bad about yourself, but not as bad as he will make you feel when he leaves the world you all have built together and moves into another one he has built for himself." That is what I would tell myself now.

And okay, so maybe I don't even want to think about my husband now. I want to dance and sing and go around the world with Sam. But if someone came up to me and said, "Pammy, you can go back now. Flick wants you to come home and he will quit seeing the slut tramp bitch," I would go back. Why? Because he is my little girl's daddy and she is more important to me than anything in the world. And I believe a little girl deserves to have her mommy and daddy together.

It's just that I hoped if I did get that call, maybe I'd get to have a quick fling with Sam first. Just a quick one. After all, I'm only human. And I'm talking about a man. I'm talking about the kind of man who leaves a woman thinking about his hands when she isn't with him. I'm talking about the kind of man who makes a woman think about sex.

14

Sam has the greatest hands. They are incredibly large. When he puts his hand over mine, he covers my whole hand up. When he reaches across the car to touch my face, it feels as if his thumb spreads out over my entire cheek. I can't help but watch his hands all the time. As he talks. As he drives. As he takes me up in a plane for flying lessons.

I never wanted flying lessons. Flying has always scared me to death. But I would have done anything with Sam. Anything. I even went so far as to go to the Delaware Water Gap to go parasailing with him. That is when you get in a plane with long, skinny wings and no motor and you glide around with the wind and when you land, you land with the wind.

Nothing made much sense to me anymore. But I did know that with Sam, I finally understood what trust was. I could see in his eyes that he had only my best interests at heart. I knew that when he took me up in a plane, I could forget everything.

All that had faded with Flick. With Flick, my interest had been a short term deal, with everything that came after, a long term deal of constantly struggling to keep him interested in me.

But Sam made me feel like everything I said and did was a lovely surprise and the surprises would never stop coming. There would always be something interesting coming out of me. And I wondered, how could one man make me feel so bad, when another man could come along and make me feel like I was queen of the world?

And then it came to me. I had married a very mediocre man. But Sam was brilliant. He was the kind of man that came along so rarely in a woman's life. He was Halley's comet.

After we flew over the Delaware Water Gap I told him so. And do you know what he said to me? He said, "Pammy, one of these days you're going to realize that it isn't me who's Halley's comet. It's you."

Now I ask you. What can you do with a man like that except try to make love to him all over the plane he is trying to fly?

Two weeks after I left Flick, two weeks of Flick making these horribly feeble calls to try and get me back, Sam took me to Atlantic City. He let me help him bring his small airplane in over the ocean and he said, "See where the sea meets the land? That's the beginning of our continent. You're flying over the beginning of America." It was right in there where I realized it was the beginning of Sam.

We landed, caught May's cab, gambled, then walked the boardwalk. The same boardwalk I had walked when I was in the Miss America Pageant. The same boardwalk where Miss Texas and Miss Montana and I had walked together, secretly hating each other just a little because there was always the chance that one of us would win out over the other one, but mostly loving the hell out of being together since nobody else in the world was as happy as we were at that exact moment. We had just had our pictures taken in one of those quick photo machines. Our tongues were sticking out. Our state sashes were tied across our foreheads in silky headbands. All of us pretended to kiss each other and smile into the camera at the same time. Three black and white photos documenting all the happiness of three beauty queens who had made it bigger than anyone they knew at the time. Or might ever know.

Sam and I passed Alabama Avenue. Then we passed Alaska, and Sam said that Alaska had more mosquitoes than any other state in the union, which I found hard to believe. He had not spent much time down south.

"You know," I said, "I'm going to have to remember to tell my Evie that. For some crazy reason, she has always wanted to live in Alaska."

We walked on, passing Colorado Avenue, Connecticut and Delaware. Then we came to Georgia Avenue and I thought about Flick, but somehow I wasn't mad at him. In a funny kind of way, I sort of hoped he was having himself a good time.

We passed Iowa Avenue and I couldn't remember the capital of the state to save my life. We passed Kansas Avenue, Kentucky and Maine and then I stopped at Montana and looked out across the black ocean and thought about Miss Montana and wondered what had happened to her.

Sam said, "You know, Pammy. If we could walk across the ocean right now, we'd end up in Morocco or southern Spain. And just think. Somebody over there is probably saying the same thing about us right now." And it came to me, that I was a very ignorant woman. There were huge gaping holes in my education. I was no more advanced in my knowledge than my little girl. What I mean to say is that up until that point, if I had lived in Morocco or southern Spain or the south of France or Russia or anywhere, I'd have still thought that if you could walk across the ocean, you'd end up in China. It never occurred to me to think any other way. In my mind, I was still a little girl digging a hole in her backyard trying to get to Peking. But now, maybe twenty-five years later, it was occurring to me that if I did dig straight down, I'd end up in New Zealand or Australia. Actually, I didn't even know where the hell China was.

But why was it bothering me now? It had never bothered me before. I'll tell you why. Because soon, my little girl was going to pass me right by. One day she was going to be as smart as her daddy and then she, too, wouldn't have anything to talk to me about. It was frightening.

Summer had arrived. Evie was officially out of school. If I began studying now, I would have three months to bone up on some knowledge while she was busy playing with her grandmother. It would give me the chance to zip ahead of her a little bit. But three months wasn't a lot when you considered the mind of a child. I wasn't stupid. I knew that if you stuck a child and an adult in school and tried to teach them the same thing, the child would speed right by while the adult was still trying to get the rules straight.

I have to admit, it had bothered me some the past year, this feeling that I was falling behind. I had always known how to help Evie with her homework before. But sometime during the last year, she had begun to come to me with these outrageous math problems which would leave me throwing my hands up in despair. How could anyone understand those problems, is what I was thinking. But eventually Evie would figure them out on her own and come to me saying,

"See, Mommy. This is how you do it." And do you think I could understand them even after she explained them to me? No.

And worse. Lately, she'd been using words I'd heard, but it had never ever occurred to me to learn to use them myself. A small little word like "vapid" would come tripping off her tongue and I'd be standing there, stunned, thinking, "Hey, wait a minute here. I don't even know what that means."

That was frightening, too.

I guess I knew she was beginning to sense a vacancy in me. An ignorance. I mean, it had even gotten to the point where she would be able to use words I knew but never knew how to use. Like the simple word "abhor." Okay. I'd be doing something, making a bed or something, and she'd walk in and say, "I abhor homework." And I'd think to myself, "Hey, now there's a word I know. But do I ever use it?" Hell, no I never use it. Why? Because I'd feel like a stupid idiot using a word like that. If I used one complex word to replace a simple word, then I'd have to start using other complex words to replace other simple words, and I didn't know very many other words. But there she was using one smart word after the other, and I knew more smart words were to follow. And was I supposed to just stand there and smile when we reached the point where she could talk but I couldn't understand?

So. What did I do? I did what any frightened mother would do. I went to the library and checked out books on how to build up my vocabulary. And suddenly I saw. No. I wasn't going to build up my vocabulary. What do I mean? I'll tell you what I mean. I could learn the damn word. It wasn't like I couldn't learn what it meant and how to spell it. But do you think I could learn how to use it? Hell, no.

Just like everything else, it stuck out like a sore thumb when it came out of my mouth.

For one thing, I couldn't find the simple hard words. It seemed to me that the only words I could find to learn were the long, hard ones like "perspicacity." I'd be sitting at the dinner table with Flick and Evie and suddenly out of nowhere I'd say something stupid like, "I'm glad I had the perspicacity to cook dinner a little later than I had planned."

Come on. I mean, everyone knows if you're going to use a word like "perspicacity," you're sure as hell not going to use the word "glad." You'd say something else. Something like, "I'm delighted I had the perspicacity to whip up this fancy little dinner later than planned." At least that was what I was thinking.

So I tried that out, and Evie said, "Mom, I'm not so sure you would use that word that way. Would you, Daddy?"

"Not exactly."

Dead silence. We just sat there and ate our peas and rice and roast beef. It wasn't even a very good dinner. I couldn't talk. I couldn't cook.

I shuddered thinking of that time as I continued to stare across to Morocco. "Sam," I said, "please don't make fun of me. But I need a favor."

"I'm not going to make fun of you, Pammy. What is it?" he said, still looking out across the ocean.

"I want to learn how to be smarter."

He kind of laughed. "You are smart."

"No, Sam. I'm not. I'm actually pretty stupid. But I'd like to try and change that. I don't want my daughter coming home from college one day just to end up sitting on the porch by herself feeling sorry for me because I'm such an idiot. Will you help me?"

"On one condition," he said, reaching over and rubbing the back of my neck.

"Anything."

"You quit knocking yourself down all the time. You are very bright. You have more potential than anybody I think I have ever met."

"No kidding? Me? The Little Miss Garden State Tomato Queen? No. I don't think so."

"Well," he said, this time taking my chin in his hands and pulling my face towards his. "I know so." He looked at me long and hard. Studied me. Then he said, "Pammy, one day, you are going to realize just how special you are. Until then, I'm going to do everything I can to get you to believe me." He kissed me, again, and for one little sparkling moment, I did believe him.

15

Miss New Jersey met me at the door when I arrived back at her house at two in the morning, fresh from Atlantic City, fresh from just falling in love with Sam. It's funny how young I felt. A little guilty for doing what I wanted. A little defiant. It was amazing to think that my baby girl was going to be reaching this stage soon. That there would come a time when she'd trample in late one night and we'd have the same face-off my mother and I were about to have. And she'd feel the same way I felt staring at my mother right then. Like if Miss New Jersey said one word, one single solitary word, I'd bite her head off.

She said, "Isn't Sam wonderful?"

This threw me. Of course, my mother liked to do that occasionally. Throw me. For instance, the day after Sam first kissed me at the Morristown Airport, when I was hungover and still desperate about Flick, she had met me at the door and said, "You missed your little girl's first hangover. The poor child was throwing up all morning and then I took her shopping and she threw up there, too. Oh, it was a sight but don't worry about it. She's the funniest little girl I know. You've raised a real fireball. She kept grabbing her head and joking, 'Nana, bring me steaks to put over my eyes.' 'Bring me ice cubes for my head.' 'You may be whispering to you, but you're yelling to me.' 'I want some hair of the dog. Give me three hairs of the dog. No, make that a hundred hairs. Forget the hairs, bring the whole dog.' I tell you, I couldn't quit laughing. Pammy. She's a livewire, that one."

Miss New Jersey had been so nice to me that day, on a day when I had really expected her to lecture me for letting everything get so out of hand. And when I had told her how badly I felt about missing Evie's hangover, she had replied, "Get over it. All mothers miss their daughters' first something horrible. Jesus, the worrying you do."

So, miraculously, my mother was able to get me through the first gaping hole I had committed in child rearing. Okay, so I had screwed up in my marriage. But my mother, my beautiful, wonderful mother, had made it sound as though I'd done something right with my child. Nothing, I mean nothing, makes a mother feel better than to know that she's taught her child how to make the best of a bad situation. And be strong through it. And be able to laugh through it. And be able to make other people laugh with her while she goes through it.

Other, more horrible mothers might have raised their children to be little whiners. But I had raised mine into a little champ.

I loved knowing my mother and daughter had spent the last two weeks together, laughing. It made me a little sad, because Evie never laughed with me anymore. But at least she was laughing with someone.

At least she was able to laugh through the breakup of her mommy and daddy.

I mean, she didn't really know about us. But she had an idea. I was sure. There was every indication in the fact that she got drunk to see that she understood something was going on. I mean, maybe if Flick and I had been holding hands in front of her she would have never had a drink at all. Instead, she would have kept pulling the cigarettes out of Flick's hands and saying, "Daddy, you shouldn't smoke. Smoking is horrible," like she used to do.

God, my little girl will probably never ever be quite as young again as she was those times when she was pulling those cigarettes out of her daddy's hand. She had finally crossed over the invisible line from believing everything could be corrected, to realizing that very few things could be corrected. She knew now that she'd just have to find ways to laugh around the uncorrectable things. What was sad, so sad to me, was that it was such a grown up way to be. And I wasn't ready for my little girl to grow up that fast yet.

I guess each time I came back from being with Sam, I expected my mother to point all this out to me, to tell me that my daughter was falling apart. Even though, as I said, she hadn't been anything but wonderful to me about Evie so far. Still, she was a mother, so I expected things to change any day. I expected it the most when I came back home that night in love with Sam. It was as if there were some universal law that if a woman was too happy while she was being dumped by her husband, everything else would break loose. So, when I came back flushed with love I said, "Sam's pretty nice, Mother."

And she said, "Sam's wonderful."

And I said, "Yes, he is. I can't figure out exactly what he does, though. He's a lawyer, but he's a pilot and he owns all these buildings and he has this auctioning thing on the side. What do you call a man like that?"

She winked at me and said, "You call a man like that a catch, darling."

I pretended to be shocked. "Yes, Mother. For a single woman."

"Well, for a married woman, you sure are seeing a lot of him. Not that I mind, mind you."

"Mother!" I said. "I'm working with Sam."

Looking back on it now, I'd have to say I couldn't have been more transparent. You'd have had to be a flaming pulsing idiot not to have seen the hormonal writing all over my walls. But at the time, I didn't want my mother to know anything about me. So I figured she didn't.

It's funny, isn't it? The way you can talk to your mother about every little boring thing when you're happily married. But the minute things go wrong, the minute you need her the most, you can't open your damn mouth.

I think Sam was right when he said if it made sense, it probably wasn't love; because, if you ask me, the greatest love in the world is the love that goes on between a mother and daughter and it never makes any sense at all.

16

I decided to take a nice warm bath. It was three in the morning, I was in love with Sam McKinnley and I had to think it over.

I could never resist my mother's bath cubes and sachets and those little balls of oil which dissolved, making the water smell like roses and gardenias. When I was a little girl, I used to take the skins of the balls that hadn't dissolved and put them on my little nipples and pretend I was a big Las Vegas stripper. I'd thrash around in the water, doing a little belly dance, which would usually end up with me kicking Joe's soap on a rope off the spigot. That would end that. I wasn't supposed to ever touch anything that belonged to him.

There was a time before Joe arrived, when it was just me and Miss New Jersey. I'd sit in the bathroom and watch her prepare for her day. Bath powder would float in the ray of sunlight that came in through the window over her tub. Her pink fluffy mules would match my pink fluffy mules which matched the pink fluffy toilet seat cover and the pink fluffy bath mat and all the little pink heart shaped soaps that were everywhere.

Those were the times when I would sit on the edge of her tub and she'd say, ''Now, Pammy, I'm going to show you something my mother showed me, and hopefully one day you'll show your daughter the same thing. This is how you take care of yourself when you get out of the bath.''

She'd rise out of the tub, completely naked, and tenderly pat the front of her beautiful beauty queen body with a towel. Then, she'd turn around and rub her shoulders and back ferociously. Then, slipping the towel even lower, she'd do an even more ferocious fanny cha-cha-cha. At which point, she'd put the towel between her legs and do another cha-cha-cha and say, ''Now, don't forget this part. This is the most important part.''

After she climbed out of her bath, she always wrapped her hair in a pink turban which matched the pink robe she wrapped herself in and she'd head out the door. And not one day went by when she didn't turn back and ask, ''Pammy, you didn't forget to do your job this morning, did you?''

My job. No wonder I was messed up.

Well, those were the days when my mother was my mommy. When I'd already been voted the Garden State Pretty Baby and the New Jersey Tiny Tot, but when I hadn't quite figured out what it meant, or what having a mother named Miss New Jersey meant. To me, at that time, she was my warm, sweet mother. No matter where I sat my little legs barely touched the floor and my skinny little arms were always held out to her. And then one morning I woke up and saw a large square green soap on a rope with a picture of a ship etched into it, dangling from the tub faucet, breaking the spell of my mother's soft pinkness forever. It was as if somebody had thrown a baseball through a rose window.

After that, I was always taking my baths alone, with the door locked, trying to cover my private parts the best way I could with my pink washcloth in case Joe decided to walk in on me. But no matter how I arranged that small square of cloth, he was going to catch an eyeful of something if he walked in. I could never get it to cover up everything. Of course, he never did walk in, but I often wondered if when Evie took her baths in my mother's bathtub, if she did the same thing with those pink washcloths. That was the kind of man her grandaddy Joe was. The kind who you always figured would probably burst in on you while you were bathing.

I held my nose and went completely under the water, watching my hair float around me. When I came up, it stuck to me, covering my body as though it were seaweed. Then I noticed that Joe's soap on a rope was no longer hanging from the faucet.

Well, the only other thing besides golf and Jackie Gleason that my mother and Joe had in common was that everything was a constant with them. Nothing changed. If he used soap on a rope when he was in the army, he was going to use soap on a rope for the rest of his screaming life. So, where was his godforsaken soap on a rope? Immediately I thought Evie had taken it. But she wouldn't have done that, because, for one thing, she hated the little Grandaddy Joe chest hairs that were always stuck on it. Maybe he just forgot to hang up a new bar?

But that wouldn't have been like him either. I got up and tiptoe dripped across the pink rug to the pink linen closet and there were no soap on a ropes to be seen anywhere. No ten-for-two-dollars cheapo generic razor blades to be seen either. And no he-man deodorants or Brut after-shaves.

The place was marvelously free of him.

Maybe my mother had moved him out to his workroom. It wasn't as if he couldn't live out there. He was always building things with electrical parts and plumbing connections. Strange light fixtures, which had been picked up off the side of a road, blasted out of his workroom ceiling with wires going in all directions. The light that came from them was a low wattage, dully lighting up the golf clubs that rested on the old, torn pool table Joe had proudly paid fifty dollars for at a garage sale. In fact, he had never paid more than fifty dollars for anything he had, up to and including his old station wagon, which carried around all the other things he'd bought for fifty dollars or less, or picked up off the side of a road.

He was a true Renaissance man. He could put together anything—as long as it didn't have to look good. He had even gone so far as to build himself a little shower unit on the back of the house, which looked an awful lot like, well, like a shower unit somebody had built on the back of a house. Somebody, that is, who didn't know what they were doing.

There was my mother's perfect Cape Cod house, with Dutch iris lining her walkway like women in a bathing suit competition. Peonies lining the house as if they were lining up for the best evening gown. And then that contraption, looking like a bunch of old golf clubs twisted together sticking out of the back of Miss New Jersey's house, as if Joe had come along and my mother could no longer hide her slip. It had started to show.

God, would my life end the same way? I'd think one thing, but actually something completely different would be happening to me. I mean, surely my mother must have thought Joe was something else in the beginning, or why else would she have married him? What else could she have ever seen in him?

Or maybe more to the point, what did I ever see in Flick?

17

If there was ever a beauty pageant to be entered, Miss New Jersey would be the first to sign the entry form. So, there was no hesitation when she brought home the forms for the Miss New Jersey Legacy of Beauties—a mother–daughter–granddaughter beauty contest—and signed them for us. Without even asking. I came down for breakfast the next morning and suddenly I got a flash as to how Evie must have felt all those times she had yelled at me, "All right. I'll do it. But couldn't you have at least asked me about it first?"

"Mother, I don't have time to enter a pageant," I said.

"And why not? This is with your daughter, Pammy. How often do you get to do something like this with your own daughter? You just sit right down there and think about it while I go get some fresh bagels for us."

I thought about it. There were problems, of course. For one thing, we'd have to keep Evie from shaving her eyebrows off again. We'd have to keep her away from razors completely. She was going to whittle herself away. Somehow during the middle of the night, she had managed to shave a square inch of hair completely off above her right ear. Just another flashing neon sign of puberty. And okay, so I could have slapped a wig over it or gotten her other hair teased around to cover it up. But that wasn't the point. The point was that she had done it. What on earth had made my little girl stand in front of a mirror and hate herself so much that she would do something so ugly? First, her eyebrows, then part of her hair. Soon it would be all of her hair.

She sat down, rubbing her eyes and said, "Where's Nana?" Not "Good morning, Mommy," or "I love you, Mommy," or even "How's it going, Mom?"

I said, "Evie, that is the worst thing I've ever seen anyone do to their hair. You look awful."

"Why, thanks, Mom. I really appreciate that."

And naturally when my mother returned with the bagels, she threw her hands up in the air and clapped. "Fern, that is the cutest little haircut I've seen in years. You know, your mother once cut off her hair to match her Barbie doll's and she ended up looking like she'd gotten her hair caught in a car motor. She was a living fright." She reached over and patted Evie's bald spot tenderly and added, "But then, she never did have the talent you have." She turned to me. "Isn't it precious, Pammy? It's so modern!"

Little Fern made a snide face at me and said, "Yeah, Mom. Isn't it precious?"

Miss New Jersey pulled some lox out of the refrigerator and put it on the table next to the bagels. "You know, Fern, when Tangerine, here, was nine years old she got it in her head to shave her legs and she didn't use soap or water. The poor thing was bleeding all over the place. I could a died, I tell you. She had to do a bathing suit contest the next week

and there wasn't a thing to do but put Band Aids and
medications all over her scrawny shins and hold my breath.
But even that didn't work, so I ended up having to put
skin-colored tights on her that sagged at the knees. Imagine
tights under a bathing suit. She looked horrible. Just horrible. You know, I used to think she was trying to put me in
an early grave.''

"Mother," I said, "I never cut my own hair. That was
that stupid girl down the street who did that. And for your
information, it was a pageboy she gave me, which just so
happened to be the newest style at the time."

She winked at Evie and said, "That's right. If it was in
style, Tangerine just had to have it. To this day I'm still
finding elephant pants and bell bottoms and granny glasses
in my attic."

Joe walked in from the back porch, swinging an imaginary golf club, saying, "Eh? Eh?" as if he had been giving
his famous join the army, grow hair on your chest speech to
imaginary people. Uncle Donald got up from his cedar bed
and began barking at him. But Joe was too busy making his
famous coffee to pay any attention to the dog. This was how
Joe made coffee. One jar, eight spoons of J.F.G. instant
coffee, hot tap water, shake and drink. Yukko.

As always Miss New Jersey ignored Joe, so he immediately zeroed in on Evie. "A good day's work never hurt
anybody, eh? Eh? When I was a boy, I'd walk nine miles to
school then walk home and bring in the cows for my father.
It was a hard life but we never went hungry. We never had
time to play like you young kids. We worked all the time."

"Joe," Miss New Jersey said, pushing him out of the
room, "enough." We could still hear him talking after she
closed the door. "I think," she said, turning back to us as if
he had not been there, "that we have a very good chance of
winning this contest. Don't you?"

I did. I knew we'd win. I knew what it took to show and I knew what the judges were looking for because once I had been a judge.

Here is what that was like: I arrived. It was a week-long pageant where volunteers had to surround me to keep the parents from paying me off to vote for their kids. I will not say what state it was in, but I will say it was a state where practically everyone drove Cadillacs and Lincoln Town Cars. Imagine. A shiny Town Car drives up. A tiny little girl wearing a thousand-dollar dress jumps out. She's no older than three but she has the hair of a thirty-year-old. The fat arm that holds the door open for her belongs to a woman with flat greasy hair, huge thighs, short shorts and flip-flops. It is her mother. She looks like all the other mothers.

Now, I'm not saying that every parent who enters their child in a beauty queen competition needs a miracle makeover, but I am saying that it took me being a judge to notice that most of them did. Before that, I was always too involved with the way Evie looked to notice anybody else.

The parents weren't great, but the little girls were beautiful. I'd have to say that most of them were beautiful. But there was this one little girl who was just about the ugliest thing I had ever seen. Her hair was flat and dull. Her dress was nothing. Her shoes were scuffed. But I had never seen talent as good as that in my life. Not before, not during that particular talent show, not after. So, even though her dress dipped in the back; even though she picked at her legs during her interview; even though she wiggled around while she was being introduced, I gave that girl first place for talent. Of course, she lost the title to a little girl who couldn't sing or dance but who looked like a real beauty queen.

Afterwards this fatso with hairs sticking out of his T-shirt came up to me with the ugly little girl and said, "What about my daughter?"

And I said, "What about your daughter?"

And he said, "Why didn't she win?"

And I said, "She did win. She won talent. She's marvelous in her talent."

And he said, "Yeah, I know that. But what about the beauty?"

Well, my mother and my daughter and I had the beauty and we could win this Legacy of Beauties pageant. There was always the possibility that it could make Evie and me closer. I mean, if she thought I was hell to work with, she hadn't seen anything until she worked with my mother. After that, she'd come flying at me with her arms spread wide, pleading for my love and understanding. And, of course, I would be there with that love, even though she had done nothing but turn her back on me lately.

And I can't explain where this reasoning came from or how I got it, because Flick had made it perfectly clear through his phone calls that all of this beauty pageant mess had been an embarrassment to him, but something told me that if we did win, which we would, Flick would come racing up here to get us. I'd send him a news clipping of his perfect family, happy without him, and he'd look over at that sour-faced Audrey in bed with him, her bony, undefined legs sticking out from beneath my bedsheets like number two pencils, and he'd miss us. Oh, he would miss us so much.

When I left Flick a few weeks back, the beauty queen world had seemed so trite. And compared to a marriage failing, it was. But if a pageant could pull that marriage back together, if it could show Flick what he was missing, if it could pull him back to my heart, if it could pull my daughter closer to me, then it was far, far more significant than trite. After all, didn't being a beauty queen stand for something? Wasn't the image about family? And okay, so maybe it was a little screwy. I could flip a baton or play a little Mozart on the piano or sing a little something from *Madame Butterfly* and no matter how brilliant I was, in the end it would all come down to what my heinie looked like in a one-piece. After all, if you go up on a runway, you're going up there as a beauty queen, not a brain queen. But still, behind all that bosom is the idea of the American family. And I know I romanticized it, but when your husband has fallen in love with another woman and left you to try not to fall in love with another man, so that you can be there for your husband when he decides that the woman he fell in love with is not so great after all, then you will grab at just about anything to get him back.

I just hoped and prayed Flick would discover he needed me, before I discovered I didn't need him. I prayed he would hurry. Because I tell you, a lot can happen in one summer.

18

A lot started happening right away. How did it start? The way most things start, with one mother making plans for everybody else. As always, it was my mother. The woman was mad with planning.

"It is going to take us the entire summer to prepare for this contest. Can you get away from him for that long?"

I was pretty sure when she said "him" that she meant Flick, because she said it so ugly. So I made her say his name out loud. "Who?"

"That creepy husband of yours, that's who."

"Flick?"

"Yes, of course, Flick."

"Mother, I keep telling you, he's spending the summer studying for his comprehensive exams. Don't you ever listen to anything I have to say?"

"Not if it has to do with him."

125

"Well, for your information," I lied, "he will probably come up for a visit soon."

"Yeck," she said.

"You made your point a long time ago, Mother. Now, what I'm worried about is the legal side of this pageant. Evie and I aren't exactly New Jersey residents anymore."

"Darling, I've already discussed this with Sam. He said not to worry about a thing. He's going to pull a few strings for us."

How odd to hear her call him "Sam." How odd to hear her say his name at all. But it would have been strange to hear anybody say his name, because just hearing it made me blush.

Of course, Miss New Jersey wasn't paying attention. She was too busy filling in every June, July, August date on her calendar with things for us to do. There wasn't a step we'd be able to take which wouldn't be a preparation beauty queen step. She wanted us to think crown, walk crown, sleep crown.

She even wanted us to start wearing summer gloves. She laid out some fine ecru lace gloves she planned on giving Evie. But she gave me her short white button wrist ones. They were handmade gloves, made over a hundred years ago. She said, "Pammy, my grandmother gave these to my mother when I began to enter womanhood. And my mother gave them to me when you began to enter womanhood. And now that Evie's beginning to enter womanhood, I want you to have them. And when Evie has a little girl, they should be Evie's gloves. Go ahead. Put them on."

I liked the idea of wearing them. But they felt so strange on me—as if I were missing a hat, a square pocketbook and a cute little summer wool dress. I said, "Thank you, Mother. I'll wear them sometime."

"They're for you to wear all the time when you go out.

Our dead mothers are watching us. They meant for us to wear the gloves so we'd know they were holding our hands and looking out for us. They're good luck."

Oooo. Spooky. The idea of our dead mothers looking down on everything we did. I said, "Mother, I can't wear these all the time. They'd drive me crazy."

"Well, at least try them, Pamela. And make sure to wear them during the pageant. Nobody else will be doing anything as creative or stylish. We're sure to win."

Like I said, I knew what it took to win a crown. And summer gloves weren't it. But a mother knows what's best for her child and no matter what age you are, you will always be your mother's child. So, I got to where I could wear the gloves around the house. Sometimes. But what I could not tolerate, and what seemed to be inevitable in spite of my protests, were her plans for working my little Evie over.

I mean, by the second day, she was talking plastic surgery.

"No!" I yelled. "I am not having my daughter's nose fixed!"

"Be realistic, Pammy," Miss New Jersey yelled back. "You know yourself it looks too much like Flick's nose. It needs to be bobbed or something. It's too flat. Too wide."

"It is not! She has a perfect nose. This is ridiculous."

"She's a beautiful little girl. But if you think she's got a perfect nose, you need to get your eyes checked. There's a little inbredness quality in that nose. I'm telling you, Pammy, somewhere down the line, Flick's mother married her brother or something."

"No. N, period, o, period. No. No nose job."

"Okay," she said, turning away. "But let's at least get

some liposuction to those thighs. She's got Flick's thighs. They are getting so big. So chunky.''

"Mother, they're cute thighs. They aren't chunky, either. They're athletic.''

"Athletic, smathletic. They won't do her a bit of good. I'm telling you, she's going to have a hard time in a few years buying pants that will get around those Outlaw gams. I can just take her down to Dr. Schwartzman and have them done in a day. She'll never have to worry about a thing again for the rest of her life.''

"Look, Mother,'' I said, whispering now. I was afraid Evie might walk in and hear us talking. "Evie doesn't need anything except a nice little haircut and a new gown. That is all. I'm not going to listen to any more of this.''

Silently, Miss New Jersey began to clean up the breakfast dishes. She was very quiet, but I could hear from her plotting and planning with each dish she took to the sink that she wasn't finished talking yet.

The next morning Miss New Jersey put a full plate in front of me at breakfast. I could see something coming. Usually, I got the diet platter from her. One hard-boiled egg with a slice of tomato and a lettuce leaf for breakfast. Add a low-cal slice of wheat toast. Sometimes, on a special day, like yesterday, I might get lox and a bagel. But this was different. Two fried eggs, four bacon strips, plus a bagel with cream cheese. I'd thought she was preparing Joe's breakfast, but when she laid it out in front of me, I knew for a fact she had more to say about Evie.

"Okay, Pammy,'' she started, "maybe no on the thighs, but surely you cannot deny she needs breasts. The girl is going to need breasts.''

I pushed my plate away. "Mother! She's just a kid. She hasn't even had time to develop her own.''

"Dear, I saw Flick's mother that Christmas. The woman was as flat as her hair. She's so flat that at ninety she won't even sag. She'll still perk up like a teenager. Trust me. The girl's going to need a boob job."

"Oh, brother. I suppose you'll be telling me next that she'll need her eyes widened and her cheekbones lifted and we'll have to get her a chin implant, right? Am I right?"

"Don't be irrational, Pammy. She's a beautiful little girl. However, it might not hurt to think about getting her ears pinned back. Now that's something we could do right now, today."

Evie walked in rubbing her eyes. The morning was about the only time she didn't wear black. She usually wore one of Flick's T-shirts and I could see her little knees. Those little knees just drove me crazy. She was so perfect. I didn't know what my mother was talking about.

"I need to get my ears pinned back?" she said. She looked disturbed. "Am I ugly?"

Miss New Jersey flipped her hand at her. "Nothing on you, Fern, is ugly. I was just telling your mother that if we pinned your ears back, they'd be a little prettier is all. They just seem a little too low for your face."

Too low! Great. Now my daughter would always think her ears were deformed. No matter how her grandmother had said it, Evie would always remember that her grandmother had said, "Evie, you have ugly ears." Just like she'd always remember Kenneth Knight telling her once on the playground at elementary school that she had a bubble butt. Just like she'd always remember that time when Macayla Irvin told her that her upper lip was a little too small. Just like I remembered a horrible, oily judge coming up to me once after a contest, saying, "Honey, if you weren't so long in the trunk, I'd have given you the crown."

These were the people that stuck out in our mind. These were the events that we never forgot. When we're just innocently standing there, minding our own business, not even thinking about our anatomy and someone reaches out, pings our underarm with their index finger and says, "I never noticed how large your arms were?" That would be enough for us to never wear a sleeveless shirt again.

Well, my little girl didn't need that. She already felt ugly enough as it was. And now she had to worry about her darling little ears. Now she would spend the rest of the day and all of the days after that staring in the mirror in horror at them, wondering why she'd never noticed they were too low before when obviously they had been too low for a very long time. Dropping down and lining up with her too-thin top lip.

The incredible thing was that Miss New Jersey wasn't even aware of what she had done. While she was busy washing dishes and looking at whatever was ahead of her, Evie was standing still in the present dealing with the damage done and I was speeding backwards into the past reviewing all my damage. I did not want to do to my little girl what my mother had done to me.

For instance, I could not open a can of food without thinking I was going to get botulism. With my mother it had always been: stick your ear up to the can as you open it. If any air escapes, throw the contaminated can away immediately. If you don't hear anything, then boil the contents of the can for ten minutes before you eat it. If you didn't die, then the can was okay.

Many times my mother would boil something until the pot was ruined. Then she'd stick the pot on the back porch along with all the other burnt pots she called her "pots in disgrace."

And heaven forbid if I ever ate rare meat. I had been

trained to buy the best meats at the most reputable, expensive meat markets, and then bring them home and burn them up. With meat, you cooked it at 400° for at least two hours, no matter how many pounds were in the oven, and if it still wasn't charred, you could bet your bottom dollar that trichinosis was in there just waiting to kill you.

I probably came from a long line of fatsos, but just stayed skinny because my mother had taught me at an early age that I could die from just about anything I ate.

And that was only the food damage.

The real damage came with my sexuality. I mean, there I was happily being my little four-year-old self, and I guess I had both of my hands under the cover and the cover was moving or something, and Miss New Jersey came in and said, "What are you doing? You're not supposed to be playing with yourself." And now I know she was wrong, because it is okay to play with yourself, but when you're a little girl you don't know that. All you know is what your mother tells you. So for the longest time afterwards, I wouldn't touch myself down there. Except, of course, when I visited my grandmother's house, because she had an old-fashioned clawfoot bathtub with a green hose attached— the kind that is supposed to have a sprayer on the end of it, but there wasn't a sprayer on hers, just a tube—and even I, living under the shadow of death when I ate, and deformity when I masturbated, even I couldn't resist that tube. And now that I'm older, I'm wondering why she didn't have that sprayer attached to that wonder tube herself.

And I won't even go into my period, except to say that my mother wouldn't let me use Tampax and the first time I had ever seen a feminine napkin was on my semiretarded assistant choir director at camp, and afterwards I always associated it with being handicapped. So you can only imagine how I felt when I came home one day from school and saw that blue box with the blossoming white flower on the front propped up against my pillow. I'll tell you how I felt. I felt as if God hated me.

But it wasn't God who hated me. It wasn't even my mother who hated me. If anything, it was her mother who hadn't hated her at all but had just been taught by her mother, who had been taught by the mother before her, that we were supposed to hate ourselves for being women.

Goodness. Grandmothers, mothers, daughters.

And add the element of the beauty queen to that and you've got two plus two equals a lineage of really fucked-up women.

Suddenly I got this huge flash that I had spent my life looking into a spoon for a reflection, instead of a mirror. Nothing ever looks good enough to the beauty queen. Everything is there, but a little off. White trash may have had good teeth, but beauty queens are long in the gum or one tooth is longer than the other or brighter than the other or dimmer than the other. Our faces distort when we least expect it. Our hair can be a foot tall, but it is never tall enough. Our eyes need to be bigger. Our ears smaller and pinned back. We are not normal people who look good. We are strange women who never look good enough.

And did I want my little girl to spend the rest of her life looking into that spoon?

Once there was a time when she was being interviewed by a judge. This judge was pushing seventy, but you could tell that she wasn't having any of it. She was wearing a pink, frilly little girl's dress and purple tennis shoes and she had on bright red glasses to offset any age that had managed to creep through. And Evie walked in and said, "Those are interesting glasses."

And the woman got all excited and said, "Oh! Do you like them?"

And Evie said, "I wouldn't wear them."

What a brassy little girl she had been. But now that had all changed. Now she was standing in front of my mother with my mother essentially saying the same thing to her about her ears that Evie had said to that judge about her glasses, "I wouldn't wear them." And I could tell she was already well on her way to looking for her reflection in that spoon.

She shrugged her grandmother off and came over to me and rested one of her ugly little ears against my shoulder. For the first time in weeks she let me hug her. I used to hug her all the time. She was my little flower and I could water her and pull the weeds out from around her and feed her and watch her grow and thrive. But one day she let the weeds take over. She wouldn't let me pick them fast enough. And then I couldn't get through them to help her anymore. It was always up to her, now, to turn my way so I could shine some light on her pretty little face.

"Honey, you have beautiful ears," I said, whispering softly, rubbing her tender head. Her hair smelled like a small kitten's breath.

"No, I don't," she said. "I have ugly ears. They look ludicrous."

"Ludicrous" out of the mouth of my child and I didn't even know what it meant. How was I supposed to respond? Where did she get these words? I was still running to the dictionary to look new words up that I could use, only to find "cotyledon," which meant something like the first seminal element of germination. How was I supposed to soothe my daughter's soul with that? I didn't even know what "seminal" meant.

I just hugged her tighter and tried to hug the ugliness away. And for a split second there, for a wonderful little moment, she gave in to the hug and melted into my arms the way she used to when a stranger came up to us in the grocery store and said, "What a beautiful little girl she is."

And she was a beautiful girl. There was no question that she was beautiful, except in her mind, and unfortunately that was all that really mattered. She pulled herself away and left me holding all her beautifulness in my arms, while she took all her ugliness alone with her to her room.

19

I didn't hear it at first. And then I did hear it. Or I thought I heard it. But then I listened for it and didn't hear it again. So I stuck my ear up to my old bedroom door just to be sure, the way my mother had probably stuck hers up to it so many times before, and then there wasn't any question. My little Evie was crying.

She'd been crying all day. It had started not long after she'd gone to her room. Then I had followed. Then she had yelled, "Get out of here, you witch! I hate you. I don't want to ever see you again. Get out! Get out! Get out!"

A few hours later I went back in and she screamed even louder. Then I tried it again, and again it was worse. Suddenly, and for the first time in her life, I didn't know how to help her.

This time, it was different.

It wasn't as if she'd fallen off her bicycle or some kids had beaten her up at school or she'd lost a pageant. My little girl was losing a lot more than a pageant this time. She was turning thirteen soon and losing her childhood and in the process, she was losing her mommy and daddy. At least that was what she thought.

I wanted to take her in my arms and say, "Oh, honey, you're not losing your daddy. He'll always be your daddy. And you'll never lose your mommy, because I'm going to be here for you long after you need me." But I couldn't say that, because for one thing, I hadn't been there for her. I'd gotten sloppy and begun to roll in at all hours of the morning after having been with Sam, sneaking into the bed next to her, trying not to wake her. And obviously she'd been waiting up for me the whole time.

How did I know? I'll tell you how I knew. Because I was that little girl's mother and the tears I was hearing behind my old bedroom door were the same tears I had cried when my mother let me down; they were the same tears I had cried when I had hated my mother so much for sending my real father away.

And I never even knew my father. But I had hated her so much that I knew why he'd gone. He'd gone because she was the most horrible woman on earth. Who could love her? Why had he married her? Why had he left me with her? Hadn't he known that I would be just as miserable with her as he'd been?

It was hours later when I put my back against that door and listened to my daughter cry. I slid down slowly, until I was sitting on the floor, paralyzed, wondering when she was ever going to stop. Wondering how such a little girl could cry for such a long time.

20

I wondered if my mother had ever felt paralyzed with me. If she had, she had never shown it. I've never seen anyone quite so coldblooded.

I'll never forget how she acted when I got pregnant my first time. Thirteen and abortions were illegal and I'd been sneaking out to meet some creepo in a trailer park just so I could have somebody to love me. I didn't even know what sex was. It did not even occur to me that it had anything to do with anything except my breasts until I did it.

Up until that time the only boyfriend I'd ever had was fat old Mary Louise Palance. Only she wasn't so fat then. She was this skinny little kid and I was this skinny little kid and we'd both grown just enough breasts to worry about them not growing any more. We started out by drawing naked women on Saturday mornings with things dripping out of their nipples. Not long after that, we began playing boyfriend and girlfriend, where we'd put a Kleenex over our mouths and kiss each other. She had bad breath.

Pretty soon, we had graduated to boss-secretary, where we'd always fight over who got to be the secretary, because if you got to be the secretary then you didn't have to wear a shirt and you got to be courted. We must have spent a half a year's worth of Saturdays chasing each other around the room, trying to touch each other's breasts. Because the breasts were the thing. Everybody knew that. Hell, the whole reason we stopped being friends had to do with our breasts. Our mothers gave us money to go to Bamberger's to buy bras and the saleswoman gave me a training bra, but gave Mary Louise a 32-A and I just wasn't in her league anymore. I mean, everybody knew that all you needed to get a man was a pair of 32-A's. And damn, that Mary Louise lorded those things over me.

So, there I was, thirteen, removing that training bra for Marvin, my trailer park lover, getting the shock of my life. Because up until that time, I had always thought the other thing was only used for a tee-tee. And that sex had to do with the breasts.

That is how young I was.

I was so young, in fact, that the first time I really made out with him, I mean, really rolled around on the floor kissing him, I thought we had done it. I was so green, that after we really did do it, I thought I was pregnant. And of course, I wasn't.

But it wasn't long after that, that I was.

God, it all happened so fast. What a strange time.

I listened to Evie's cry, so soft and hopeless, and I almost wished she had been pregnant. Pregnant, I could have helped. When I was a child I used to think that if my child ever got pregnant I would grab her up and say, "Tiffany," because when I was thirteen that is what I had planned to name my baby, "Tiffany, you just close your eyes and hold my hand and your mommy will get you through this." When I was thirteen, my baby was going to have the nicest life. I was going to be her best friend and when she was old enough, we'd shop together and wear each other's clothes. It never even occurred to me that I might have a boy.

A lot of things didn't occur to me back then. I was just so happy that I was finally going to have somebody of my own I could love back the way I had never been loved. I didn't think about finances or trailer parks. I was too busy thinking about getting married and going to Woolworth's to pick out plates and spoons. It was really an exciting time for me. Finally I could have the kind of family I always saw on television.

Then I got really sick. Miserably sick. I couldn't eat anything and everything I could eat I threw up and suddenly I didn't want to be pregnant anymore. I didn't want to marry Marvin anymore. I didn't even want my daddy back. I just wanted to be normal again, without Miss New Jersey ever finding out that I hadn't been.

So, I did everything I could to give myself an abortion. I exercised. A lot. I drank gallons of water. I took boiling hot baths. I swallowed quinine tablets. I beat my stomach. But still, still I remained pregnant.

So, what did I do? I did what any thirteen-year-old girl with a solid mother would finally do. I told her.

And do you know what she said to me then? I'll tell you what she said. She said, "Pammy, how could you do this? The Miss Teen Apple Pageant is coming up next month."

Or, at least that's what I remember her saying. She says she didn't say anything like that. She says the way she remembered it, she asked me who the boy was.

So, I told her. Marvin was her car mechanic. Her car was always breaking down and she was always making me go with her to the repair shop and there are only so many Tabs a prepubescent girl can drink at a gas station before she gets bored.

Miss New Jersey wouldn't go with me to the doctor. She sat in her car and made me go alone. He was a chiropractor with shiny, greasy hair, and I can still remember being on that table with him examining me, feeling that shiny, greasy hair on the back of my thighs.

And that song, "I Never Promised You a Rose Garden," was being piped out through the Muzak. I remember that.

Evie had quit crying for a minute. But when she started back up, she was closer to the door. She wasn't coming out. I knew exactly what she was doing. She was standing at the dresser, looking at herself in the mirror. And she was probably looking at the pictures of me as the Miss Teen Apple Queen, hating me because I had been so beautiful when I was her age. She would look at my thick brown hair, barely touching my slim shoulders, wishing she had brown hair, not knowing that when I was her age I would have killed for blond hair like hers. She'd look at the pictures of me, smiling with my mother, my mother's arm around me, and she'd wonder why her mother wasn't as wonderful to her.

She wouldn't know, and she didn't need to ever know, that my mother didn't speak to me for two solid months after my abortion. For two solid months, if she needed us to communicate, she did it through notes. I hadn't thought I was bad before the abortion, and I hadn't thought I was bad through it. But when my mother shut down on me, I thought I was the most horrible kid in the world.

Well, when I look back on it now, I wish I could have hugged myself and said, "Oh, Pammy. Look how neat you are. How lovable you are," because I was and nobody else was hugging me that way.

There had been another woman waiting with me in the back room of that chiropractor's office. A beautiful brunette woman, like my mother, only sadder. She seemed so old to me back then, but she was probably as old as I am now. She was crying like she was never going to stop. I kept saying, "Please don't cry. Everything is going to be fine." But she just kept crying anyway. The way my little Evie kept crying now. Only it wasn't as sad as Evie's cry. It was just more beaten down. I don't know.

She had taken my little thirteen-year-old hand and said, "If we just didn't do that one thing in our lives. One thing! If I just hadn't drunk that bottle of Thunderbird. I hate my husband. I don't even want to be married to him. Johnson's car smelled like new leather. It just made me crazy. It made me wild." She was babbling on through her tears, a string of confetti sentences, one this color, one that color, another another color, never really matching, but all saying the same thing—that she was unhappy and scared.

"It'll be okay," I said again, patting her on the back.

It's funny what you can remember when you're listening to your own daughter cry and you're trying to put yourself in her place. You remember the small details about how you were when you were her age. I don't remember if the doctor was mean or nice. He was just there. I don't remember walking out of the building. Or getting home. Or my mother when I got home. But I do remember that I was sitting beside that woman, telling her things would be fine, watching my little legs kicking my brand new Keds back and forth, back and forth. I thought they were the prettiest shoes. And isn't it odd for a little girl to carry a memory like that with her through all these years? Because I tell you, we think we are so old when we're thirteen, but I must have, somewhere in the back of my mind, seen my little shoes and known that I wasn't as old as I had thought I was.

But sometime not long after the abortion, I was with my mother at the Jersey shore, with her not talking to me, and I was running along the beach as it was getting dark and it came to me just how old I'd become.

I didn't want my daughter to feel that old yet.

The last thing the nice brunette at that clinic had said to me was, "Where's your mother?"

"She's out in the car. She didn't want to come in."

"What about your boyfriend?" she had asked.

"He's gone."

"Did you love him?"

"I don't know. I guess so. We were going to get married. He played the guitar and wrote love songs for me."

Then she began to cry again. "I can see why you wanted to have a child. Poor little girl."

Then I reached out and held her hand again, and again I said, "It's going to be okay. I promise. Tomorrow the sun's going to come up just like it always does and you're going to be a brand new person. Just watch."

God, I really like that little girl I used to be. All alone, turning into a grownup, comforting a grownup who had turned into a child. So, why didn't I like her then? And why the hell don't I like the grownup version of her now? Will I wake up in twenty years and think I was a wonderful mother when I remember this—sliding down my bedroom door listening to my little girl cry and not wanting to go in there because I am too scared to face her?

God, I used to think I had the worst mother in the world, and now my little girl comes along after all these years to show me that no mother could be as bad as I was. I had to change that. I wanted to be the mother for her that I had wanted to be for Tiffany when I was thirteen. It was time to explain to her about Flick.

I stood up, slowly, my knees cracking as I did. I listened

once more through the door. The crying had finally stopped.
I knocked lightly. She didn't answer. I knocked again. She
still didn't answer. So I opened the door.

She was laying in her bed, the sheets pulled up tight
around her neck, and she smelled like my perfume. She
must have sprayed some on right before she went to sleep.
She was my little blossom, sleeping in the New Jersey
moonlight. I just couldn't bring myself to disturb her. I just
couldn't bring myself to tell her about her daddy. I walked
back out of the room, closing the door, careful not to make
it click.

21

I do not think it is so inconceivable for a woman to fall in love with a man in two or three weeks. Maybe it is not *love* love. Maybe if she were separated from him, she would not die from never seeing him again. But I think a woman can surely look into a man's eyes, kiss his lips, hold his hands and tell that he is eventually going to be somebody she might end up loving for a very long time. Maybe even for the rest of her life.

Even if she wasn't going to end up with him.

I wasn't going to end up with Sam, but I could tell I loved him.

I believe in the institution of marriage. I believe a woman and a man should stay together even if they did make a mistake. Or didn't and just grew apart. I believe children should not pay for their parents' boredoms and irritations with each other. That is why I had every intention of going back to Flick. Maybe there was a question in Flick's mind, but there was no question in my mind that we should end up together again.

I had wanted to spend some more time with Sam. But then I had heard Evie cry and I realized this part of my life wasn't about me. It was about her and getting her daddy back.

So, I took a risk and wrote Flick a letter that night. Like I said, after I'd had Evie I thought love should be a no-trick thing. But that wasn't the way it worked. I mean, I had tried to get him back by telling him I loved him and that hadn't worked. That was obvious in the fact that I was up here and he was still down there. So I didn't have anything to lose by writing him a straight trick letter. I told him I didn't think it was going to work out:

> Dear Flick,
>   Go ahead and live with that slut tramp bitch. Your daughter has never been so miserable and I just want you to know it is all your fault. You will never see her again.
>
>   Pammy
>   P.S. I am going for total custody.

Well, that is what I wrote first. To get it out of my system. But I tore it up and then I wrote:

> Dear Flick,
>   I've decided that there's something missing between us. Either I've changed or you've changed or maybe I've just noticed for the first time what you always were. I haven't stopped loving you, but I don't think this relationship is good for either one of us anymore.
>   Please call me and let's talk about Evie.
>
>   Pammy

Then I stuck it in the mailbox and held my breath. And while I was holding my breath, I went out with Sam.

And, like I said, even though I didn't think it was impossible for a woman to fall in love with a man so fast, I was hoping it would be inconceivable for me. Because when Flick did come to get me, and I had to believe he would, I didn't want to be as in love with Sam as I was.

So, I began to question everything. So what if he flew me over New Jersey in the middle of the night and said, "Pammy, you are a beautiful woman." So what if when I told him about Evie and my mother and them ganging up on me and what side would he take, he said, "Pammy, I will always be on your side." So what if, after we landed in Blairstown and sat out at the end of the runway and I showed him how to whistle with a blade of grass, he reached over and grabbed me and said, "Pammy, I am so proud of you." "Why?" "Because you are so in love with life." So what if he said these things. Did any of that give my love for him a leg to stand on?

No. How could we be in love? I mean, we had not even made love. That in itself did not make much sense to me.

He said, "Pammy, why are you so quiet tonight?"

"Sam, why don't you want to make love to me?"

"Oh, Pammy, hon. I'm going crazy to make love to you."

"Well, you never try anything. What's stopping you?"

"You. You're not ready."

"You keep saying that."

"I keep meaning it, too."

"I don't understand."

"I know you don't."

"I bet you'd make love to somebody else," I said nastily.

And he said, matter-of-factly, "Probably. But that would be different. You're special."

We sat quietly. No planes were taking off. No planes were landing. I shot up and began to walk away.

He called out, "Pammy. Come back here. Sit down."

"No!" I yelled. "I am not going to sit down with you." I was so mad at him. I didn't know why. He hadn't done a thing wrong.

I stomped off and sat behind a twin-engine Piper on the cold, wet grass, and worried about the bugs crawling up my legs. "He'd better come get me," I thought. "He'd better not let me sit out here for too long."

I sat there for a long time. Well, to me it seemed as if it were a long time. It was probably only a few minutes, but it had seemed as if it were an hour. By the time he didn't come, I was as mad as a tornado. I jumped up from where I was sitting and ran as fast as I could to tear him up.

But he wasn't there. I threw my hands up in the air and stomped my feet, mad as a bull. I screamed his name at the top of my lungs, "Saaaam!"

Then I screamed again. "Saaaaaam! Get back here, nooooooow!"

I began to run everywhere, dashing in and out and behind the planes, as mad as a woman can be who has finally found love with the wrong man. "Saaaam!"

He threw his arms around me. He held me tight. I tried to beat him off. But he wasn't having any of it. "Pammy. Pammy. Calm down. I'm here. I'm here. I couldn't find you. Where were you?"

"I hate you," I said, sounding like my daughter. "I don't ever want to see you again. I hate you. I hate you. I hate you. Take me home."

"I don't want to take you home, Pammy," he said

calmly. "I love you. Come here, sweetheart. I love you."

"No, you don't. You won't even touch me."

"I didn't want you to regret it."

"Good. Because I would have. Going with you would be the last thing I'd want to do. Now take me home."

"I don't want to, Pammy. But if you want to go, I'll take you."

"I want to go." I huffed off and climbed back in the plane and waited while he kicked around outside for a while, frustrated. Then he climbed in, too, and grabbed me and began kissing me. He said, "You know I want you." Then he was rubbing me all over, pulling at my clothes, telling me that he had to have me, that the last few weeks had felt like years, kissing me and kissing me and kissing me stronger and better than anyone had ever kissed me in my life and I was so scared I pushed him away.

I said, "I cannot do this. I've got to get home. I need to go and be by myself. I need to go and be with my daughter."

He leaned back on his seat, breathing hard. Blowing out of his mouth, evenly, to get his wind back. Then he let out a last, small breath, ran his fingers wildly through his hair, shook his head and said, "Pammy, you are going to drive me crazy."

I began to cry as we took off. It seemed as though I hadn't cried in years. I didn't ever want to stop crying. I just laid it out all over the dashboard of his plane.

When we got up to three thousand feet, Sam leveled off and put the plane on autopilot. Then he reached over and took me in his arms. I could see the lights of New Jersey below as all the small towns were coming together to make up my birth state. For the first time in my life I was falling in love with New Jersey. But I didn't want to fall in love with New Jersey, because my home was in Georgia.

My love was supposed to be with my husband.

But then Sam said the most perfect thing a man can say to a woman who has gone temporarily insane. He traced his finger from my forehead to my chin and said, "Pammy, I don't know what's going to happen to us, or where we're going to go, but I think I will always be in love with you."

22

We went back to Sam's house. He lived in Mendham, right outside of Morristown. He had these crazy, wild cloth sculptures of wild animals in the corner of his bedroom. There was a palm tree that touched the ceiling. A giraffe that ate the leaves. A zebra butting his head against the trunk. And everywhere else there were books. Not the kind of books Flick had, but books on science, history, art, art history, stories. He even had some of the junk I read. He never held anything back in the way he was and you could see that in the way he had his house.

We made love in his bed. He was very careful with me. He kept checking my face, touching my eyes to make sure I wasn't crying. I wasn't going to cry. I was very happy to be with him. At one point he stopped and said, "Pammy, you don't have to stay married to someone who doesn't love you if you don't want."

I didn't say anything. I just kissed his eyes and began

moving slowly, getting him slowly moving again. And it was nice. I have to say, it was the kind of love a woman makes where the only thing missing is that it isn't being done to have a baby. I'm not saying I wanted to have a baby with Sam. I'm just saying that when love is that perfect, I think a woman's instincts to have a baby can't help but break through.

And when it was over, he traced words on my back. Big long sentences which I had to guess. Most of them saying, "Nobody comes close to Pammy." "Pammy is the one." "Pammy makes me very happy." Then he traced something I couldn't quite get because I was falling, falling so peacefully into sleep. I tried to figure it out, but finally I gave in to the sleep.

In the morning, I figured out what he had been trying to draw, because he had drawn it in the inside of my shoe. He'd traced a heart, and inside he'd put, "Sam loves Pammy."

23

All those days when I had been Evie's age and thought nobody loved me and I'd made up somebody to love me—and now Sam was that somebody, unmade-up.

I was scared. I was trembling. Maybe I was wrong. Maybe I was in phony love. Rebound love. But I didn't care. I was just so happy again. Like how happy I was when I had first had my little Evie. When I held her up to the morning light and she had first smiled at me and I knew I was going to be a good mother and she was going to be a perfect child.

But then.

Well.

When you're ready to have babies, you know exactly what they need to be like when they grow up to survive. But when they get there, the world has changed and you've changed. And hopefully, if you were a strong enough parent, a good enough parent, most of what you tried to accomplish took. But sometimes all it takes is one mistake on your part to screw everything up.

I had made that one mistake.

I had fallen in love with Sam and in doing so, I had skipped ahead to the next section of my life while my little Evie was still back in the last section thinking about her daddy.

I don't know why I let it all get away from me so fast.

I guess it's just that since I hoped Flick and I would eventually get back together, there wasn't any point in burdening my little girl with news she didn't need to know. But then, things just happened so fast and how do you go from not telling your child that you've left her father, to just plain straight out telling her you've fallen for another man?

The answer is, you don't. You either tell her a little bit at a time and hold your breath, or you do what I did, which was to take the coward's way out. Not say a word. Hope to God she wouldn't notice that I was laughing and singing again for the first time in years.

One thing is for sure. I'd quit singing around Flick. Imagine that. Spending the main part of your life singing and dancing and twirling the baton and then allowing one man to change you so much that one day you wake up and there isn't any singing left in you.

I must have sensed that something was wrong with him. With us. With me. I must have tried to tone myself down. I guess I probably stood over my sink washing dishes for thirteen years, each new year tightening my neck and back tighter and tighter as I got quieter and quieter trying to please him. And what kind of way was that to live?

Then I jump from that to trying to be in love with two men at the same time. And that is even more tense than a bad marriage.

I still loved Flick. Of course, I loved Flick. You don't

spend the main part of your life smelling a man's undershirt
to see if it is dirty enough to be washed without loving him.
His smells were in me. His opinions. His ways.

But how do you combine one man's ways with another
man's ways? One man's big hands with another man's
hands that are not as big but are the hands of your daughter.
One man's new memories with another man's older, longer
ones that may no longer send chills up your spine, but are
surely part of the reason your spine is there. Flick had been
my backbone.

He was the first man to tell me I was good. To convince
me I wasn't crazy. And that is not a small thing. Because
most people may not know this, but most good looking
women spend a good deal of time thinking they are going
off their rocker. When you spend the main part of your days
dressing up so somebody can understand who you are, then
you've built yourself a pretty shaky foundation to stand on.
If those clothes aren't back from the cleaners on time, if the
mascara glomps up too much, if a blemish appears, oh if a
blemish appears, it is as if an earthquake has happened and
all the ugliness has come rocking through. Because, after
all, everyone knows that without the right skin, the right
clothes, the right hair, a good looking woman is nothing.
You can tell that by the way the people talk. I know if I ever
get fat one day, or become scarred, or become tired of
slipping into the beauty mask, I'm going to overhear somebody say, "Oh, it's such a shame. She used to be such a
good looking woman."

And I will just stand there with my hands up in the air,
frustrated, going, "Well, what about the other stuff? My
ideas. My opinions. The way I laugh. They haven't left.
Don't they matter?"

You see, that is the paradox of the beautiful woman. The
fact that she knows, and the rest of the world knows, that

the beauty isn't the thing; but that knowing that doesn't matter, because the beauty really is the only thing.

And did I actually use the word "paradox"? Yes. But did I use it right? I didn't know. But I didn't really care. Because what mattered was what I was saying, not how I was saying it. And if somebody came along and judged me for one or two words used wrong, then they'd be the same ones who would judge me for one or two false eyelashes put on the wrong way.

That is why I had fallen in love with Flick. He may have turned into a creep, but he had always loved me for what I was underneath. He may have pushed things at me that I could never in a million years read or understand, but at least he thought enough of me to try.

And then Sam comes along and takes up where Flick left off. Sam made me feel that yes, maybe in a million years I could read and understand those things. Where Flick had shown me that someone could love me, Sam was showing me that I could love myself.

Well, when I woke up the next morning and slipped on that shoe with "Sam loves Pammy" written inside, and I thought about Flick going to all that trouble to spray paint our names on the overpasses, that's when I realized that I was letting Sam take Flick's place in love for a while, the same way I had let Miss New Jersey take my place with my little girl.

24

Nobody can take a mother's place.

I found this out the hard way.

I think it first started when I had called home with some lame excuse as to why I had been out all night. It was the first time I had spent the night away. Evie picked up the phone. She didn't ask where I had been. She didn't say much at first. She just let me rattle guiltily on about being stuck out of town on business.

Then finally she said, "It's okay, Mom. Mom, would it be all right if I went to a party a friend's throwing?"

"What friend? You don't have any friends up here, do you?"

"I do now," she said. "Delia. She wants me to come to her house for the day. Is that okay with you?"

Well, she had asked in such a sweet little way. And she sounded so far away. And it just seemed like all I had ever said to Evie her entire life was, "No!" "Stop!" "Don't do

157

that!'' And suddenly I just couldn't stand to say that one more time. So. I let her go. And I didn't even ask where she was going. Or how old Delia was. Or did she do drugs. Or was she perhaps really a boy. Or would there be alcohol. Or would other kids bring their puberty along.

I just sat on the edge of Sam's bed and looked at my legs and thought two things. One, that I had awfully pretty legs still. And two, that my little girl needed to have some freedom. So why not start letting her have some right now. So, I said, ''Sweetie. You go and have yourself a good time.''

After all, there does come that time, doesn't there, when a mother has to let her little girl go?

Maybe. But it shouldn't be when that woman is in between her little girl's daddy and another man. Because that is the worst time. That is the time when she is saying to you, ''Look, Mommy, I'm a mess. I am not ready to go yet. If you don't get off your ass and straighten me out soon there's going to be trouble ahead.''

All the signs were there, plain as day. The way she had begun to talk back to me in front of her grandmother. The way her hair had been smelling like cigarette smoke. The way she'd begun to shrug her shoulders at just about anything I said.

There I was, thinking, ''So, what if she shrugs and tries out cigarettes and has a little mouth on her? A child has to be thirteen years old sometime. You cannot stop a child from being that.''

But I could have at least remembered what day she was going to turn thirteen.

25

June 15 was the day I took my first flying lesson. I was petrified. I hated to fly. And it wasn't as if I had never flown, because I was a beauty queen and sometimes it feels as if all a beauty queen ever does is travel. You can be crowned little Miss Pitty Pot or Miss TV Dinner and you still have to travel. But I always drove if I could get out of flying, or took the train, or worse—and I could never tell this to anyone, not even to Flick—but sometimes I even took the bus, which is the slimiest way to travel known to man. There was not a bus I took that didn't have some greaseball squeezing in next to me with some Spanish fly and bad intentions. And I tell you, I do not even know what Spanish fly is, but I know sitting beside it is better than flying any day of the week.

But Sam told me I was wrong. He started out the way everybody starts out, by whipping off all the statistics as if I had not heard them a hundred times before. Safest way to travel. Less chance of crashing than trains, boats, buses, cars. In fact, the way everyone talked, I had more chance of a car careening off the road and pinning me up against a tree growing out of the crack of a sidewalk than I did flying. Yes, yes, yes, I'd think, I've heard it all before, but I also have more of a chance of living if I'm pinned to that tree than I'll ever have diving thirty-five thousand feet straight down trapped in tons of metal.

Sam said, "Well, you like flying with me, right?"

"No," I said. "I like being with you."

"But you're not scared when you fly with me."

"Well, yes, I am, Sam. It's just that being with you outweighs the fear."

"Okay. Well, let's try and get rid of the fear."

So, he put me in the hands of Vincent Cullingsworth, a husky ex-marine who took me up for my first flying lesson. He gave me the controls, told me how to do the pretakeoff cockpit check, how to take off, how to climb to three thousand feet, and it was at three thousand feet where I began to feel safe. Where I began to think, "Well, damn. I could like this. This is nice." Vincent told me to do this, which I did, and that, which I did, and then he told me to pull as far back on the yoke as I could, which I did, which made us go up and up until suddenly we were going straight down backwards into a full stall. I let go of everything and grabbed on to his neck, screaming.

He laughed and casually took the controls and brought us out of the stall. Then he explained that if I was going to learn how to fly I had to learn how to get out of a stall first. And while he explained this, he put my hands back on the controls so I could fly over Morristown as he showed me what I would learn in the following days: Figure eights. Flying with instruments. Landing with flaps and without. The way he didn't like women.

But that was okay because I don't think women liked him either. I know I didn't. But I tell you, you don't have to like somebody to learn something from them.

After we landed and I cussed Sam out for putting me in Mr. Vincent Cullingsworth's hands, I flung my arms around him and said, "That's the best time I've ever had. It's so hard! It's so exciting! That man is such a creep!"

Sam shook his head, smiling. "Pammy, Vincent did you a big favor up there. He showed you where the fear was."

"I already knew where the fear was."

He laughed. "Listen, Pammy, he's going to make you so cocksure about stalls you won't ever be afraid to fly again."

It was only later when I understood what he was saying to me. At the time I was still too excited to really listen to anything. "I love it! I want to go up again right now."

"Hey, kid. This is only the beginning."

"It feels so strange to walk, Sam. You steer with your feet and control the speed with your hands." I was out of breath, talking like a machine gun firing.

"I know. You should try driving afterwards. It feels like you're doing everything backwards."

We went back to his house and had a celebration picnic. Cold grapes, cold champagne, cold cheese, cold Italian bread. It began to cloud up. Instead of going in, we made love in the New Jersey rain up against a big weeping willow tree by a pond with a chorus of bullfrogs around us.

By the time I got home, I was sailing through the door.

It did not even occur to me that my little girl had wedged herself in deep with the wrong crowd. The bad crowd.

But Miss New Jersey stood in the kitchen to tell me all about it. "Pammy, your daughter is beginning to get out of control. I think you're spending too much time away from her."

"What's wrong?" I asked, alarmed. "Is there a problem?"

"I think your little girl may be a problem."

I don't know what was wrong with me, but sometimes you sense that something awful is about to happen to you and the fear becomes so strong that you turn it into anger instead. I threw my arms up in frustration at my mother. "Oh? You don't say a word if she changes her name and shaves her head, but the minute I leave the house, then she's a problem. Right? Am I right? What did she do this time?"

"Nothing too bad," she said, trying to match my snotty tone. "She just stole a VCR from Macy's."

26

Evie was still dressed in black, only these were strange black clothes that didn't belong to her. Her face was still the face of a small child, but her eyes were the wild eyes of a teenager in trouble. The minute I opened the door she began to get hysterical. Her voice was pathetic, it was strangled from trying not to cry while she screamed. "Oh! Oh! Tropical update on my mom: she's turning into a tornado, coming to get me, to destroy me. She's going to rub me out just like she did to my daddy. Pretty soon I'll just be a nub."

"Shut up, you little crook," I said. I wanted to slap her, but of course, I never hit my child. But that didn't mean I didn't want to. "What was on your mind? Have you gone crazy? I didn't raise you to steal."

"I didn't raise you to steal," she mimicked me, pushing her face right into mine. She was really asking for it.

"You little snot. You are in big trouble, young lady. Big, big trouble."

"So. I don't care. You'll get me out. No sweat." She leaned back on her pillow, grinning, testing me.

I didn't know what to do, so I stood there quietly reading the court summons to myself. She didn't talk. I didn't talk. She sat on her bed hating me. I stood at the foot of the bed, hating me, too. I mean, what kind of mother raises a child to steal from Macy's? And why a VCR? Why not a sweetheart ring and a pair of jeans? Sure, the ethics would be the same, but somehow taking a sweetheart ring would be more like swiping. Whereas a VCR was just straight out-and-out stealing. Thievery.

"It says here," I said, flicking the summons with my middle finger, "that if you tear up this summons then you can go to jail."

"Tear it up," she said, shrugging her little shoulders.

"Okay," I said. "I think I'll do just that." Her eyes got very big then, as I tore it once, then twice, then again and again and again. I sprinkled the pieces all over the bedroom floor and turned to walk away.

She began screaming. "You drove him to her. He hated you just like I hate you. That's why he's with her now. Because he was hagridden. You're a martinet and everyone hates you."

What could I say to that? I couldn't. For one thing, I didn't know what the hell a martinet was. I knew it wasn't a bird, but it sounded like a bird. I got right up in her face and said, "Well, you're a little thief." Neither one of us moved.

Once again, I was standing, stupid, in front of my little girl.

I could only pretend she hadn't said that word. After all, if I hadn't understood it, then it really hadn't counted, right?

God, I could just hear Flick now, standing behind me

saying, "See, Pammy. That's what critical theorists are for. They determine the inconsistencies in language and try to find ways to work with the limitations those inconsistencies bring about."

The reason I knew he'd say that was because he'd said it often enough when we'd been in a fight. I'd say this, then he'd say that, then I'd say this and before long he'd be asking me why I had chosen this or that word in my argument. I'd say, "Flick, that is not the point. The point is, blah, blah, blah, right?" But he would say, "No, Pammy. That is not the point. The very fact that you use blah, blah, blah means that you're probably trying to say something different than you think."

I would get so confused. I'd just throw my hands up in defeat and say, "Okay, Flick. Fine. You win. I don't want to talk about this anymore."

God, I used to think I was such an idiot talking to him. And now my little girl comes along after all these years to show me just how smart I really was. I mean, someone can tell you that a lot of words mean a lot of things, but you don't have to be a damn college genius to see that the look in your daughter's eyes can narrow all the meanings down to one. Evie was petrified. I hadn't seen her look this way since she was nine years old and she'd sent a penny in to a record club to get six free records; and they'd sent a letter back saying if she didn't pay up the extra money, she was going to be sued. She'd sweated that little bit of information out for a week before she'd told me about it.

I had said, "Oh, honey. It's okay if you sent a penny in to those clubs. Everyone sends pennies in to those clubs and gets those letters. Those clubs are irresistible. Don't worry about anything. Mommy will take care of everything."

And now I was standing before her, waiting for her to ask for my help again. All she needed was to ask. All I needed was to hear it. Sometimes you have to get that much out of your child. You cannot do everything for free. You have to teach them how to work for and through some things, and intuition told me this was one of those times.

Evie wasn't having any of it. She started screaming, "Get out! Get out! Get out!" And she didn't stop until I was out the door.

I was shaking. We had never come to this before.

I went straight to the dictionary to look up "minaret." Something wasn't right. A minaret was a high, slender tower attached to a mosque. I didn't know what a mosque was. I had to look that up, too, because I was sure she wasn't calling me a tower. I felt like a thief in the night, thumbing through the pages of the dictionary as fast as I could in the dark of my mother's den so my daughter wouldn't catch me if she walked in.

Well, I was not a mosque, either, because a mosque was a Muslim temple. And if the truth be known, I didn't even know what a Muslim was really. I mean, I wasn't so stupid that I didn't know it was something religious. Hell, I knew that. But that was all I knew.

I was so damned ignorant it gave me a headache. I looked up "Muslim," which meant an adherent to Islam. And I didn't know what the fuck an adherent was or what Islam was. But I did know what the word "mutation" meant, which was a word on the same page. As a matter of fact, I was mutating as I sat there. Going through a chain reaction of stupidity, changing from stupid to more stupid to even more stupid with every word I looked up.

I'd been better off when I hadn't known anything at all. Now it just seemed as if the things I knew, I didn't know well enough or I didn't want to know.

I went into the kitchen and said, "Mother, why would Evie call me a minaret?"

She thought about it a moment. Then she said, "You must mean a martinet. She wouldn't call you a minaret because that's a tower. That would be like calling you a roof or a steeple."

So that's where I'd gone wrong. I'd forgotten to look up a word that sounded like a bird. As I left to go look up "martinet," my mother said. "Of course, I wouldn't of called you a martinet. I would of called you the exact opposite. Letting your daughter steal like that."

"I didn't *let* her steal, Mother." I tried to slam the kitchen door, but it wouldn't slam since it has one of those air pumps attached that only makes a whisper.

Being a martinet wasn't so bad. It could have been worse. She could have called me a bitch. Compared to that, being called a very strict disciplinarian was nothing. What was bad was having to run to the dictionary to figure it out. It was as though I'd been in battle and found myself fencing without a sword, hoping my opponent didn't notice.

I was getting real tired of fencing without a sword.

27

The thing is you think you do so much for a kid. You make sure they go to bed on time. You wash their clothes. You take them to the dentist and listen to them scream when they get their teeth pulled. You put the poisons way up high and make sure when they're chewing, it's not on anything dangerous like a double-A battery. But then when you think you've thought of everything, you turn around and your kid's in trouble anyway.

I missed Flick. I mean I really missed him. You don't go through disasters with a man like your kid eating clay and wallpaper without thinking about him when she was at it again. And Evie was at it again.

I was too beat down to stay in love with somebody new, when there was my family to consider. We'd been through too many things together.

Like the time Evie had turned blue and Flick and I had to rush her to the hospital because, as it turned out, she'd been eating the carpet padding. When we returned home and put her to bed, a happier, healthier three-year-old with bright pink cheeks, we looked under the rugs and realized she'd been eating the padding for weeks. I had been crushed. I had said, "Flick, what kind of mother am I not to have noticed something like that?"

Here is how wonderful Flick was to me then. He said, "Pammy, you are what most people would call a great mother. Kids are going to be kids. They're going to get into some things you won't have any control over. And if you're lucky enough, you'll be there to pick them up and dust them off afterwards."

Well, I wanted to hear him say that now. So, I called him. He answered right away. I said, "Flick, we're in trouble," and then I explained the whole story to him.

He kept saying, "Calm down, Pammy. I can hardly understand a word you're saying." I was hysterical.

When I was finished, I added, "So, you see, Flick, we've got to get back together again. I'm horrible at this alone."

He was very quiet for a moment and then he said, "Pammy, do you remember the first day Evie went to school?"

"Uh-huh," I sobbed.

"Do you remember that you didn't want to let her go? You wanted to walk with her through the schoolyard and take her to class."

"Yes, I remember."

"Okay. But remember they asked us to let Evie out at the front gate so she could make the journey alone. Remember that?"

"Yes, and I hated it. I didn't want her to go."

"But sweetheart, she had to go. Just like she had to go through this. Kids have to kind of clear a path for themselves sometimes. They wake up and their parents aren't together any longer and they think they need to find a way out of the jungle so they start hacking away at everything hoping somebody will notice they're lost. That's why she did this. Not because you're a bad mother. But because, well, because I'm a rotten husband."

How could he say that? He wasn't rotten at all. He was just messed up. I said, "Flick, you're not rotten. Maybe you just woke up and found yourself in a jungle, too, and you started hacking your way out. That's understandable. Any woman who couldn't understand that is an idiot."

Was that me talking? I'd obviously lost my head.

"Thanks, Pammy."

"Well, what do you think we should do?"

"I don't know. I guess I should come up and see this thing through with you and Evie. Then, I don't know. Separation?"

Separation! Who was talking separation?! That scared the hell out of me. I couldn't believe he had gone that far ahead of me when there I was, going backwards to get back to him. It scared me so much I said, "Separation? Why waste our time. Let's cut straight to the divorce. Did you get my letter yet?"

"No." He sounded faint and puzzled. "Do you really think divorce? This fast?" He was probably smiling gleefully.

"Oh, absolutely. Why wait?" I, on the other hand, sounded strong and sensible, but I was about to go over the edge.

And what was the edge? What would be over that edge for me? Sam?

Here is how wonderful Sam was to me.

I hopped in my car. Two o'clock in the morning and I'm speeding down Schoolhouse Lane at breakneck speed. I rolled into his driveway, no, screeched into his driveway. I

banged on his door. He answered it. I threw myself all over
him and told him all my stories. My juvenile delinquent's
story. My story of pending divorce. I screamed. I wailed. I
why-me'd all over his house, his back, his chest.

And then do you know what that man did? I'll tell you
what he did. He reached out and said, "Pammy, you haven't
told me one thing tonight that can't be cleared up by one
stiff drink and one good lawyer." He put me on his couch.
He left the room. He returned with a down comforter. He
covered me up. He left the room. He returned again, this
time with a shot glass and a bottle. He poured me a drink
and held me up while I sipped it. I said, "God, this stuff is
great. What is that? It tastes like licorice swirls."

He winked at me and said, "Pammy, remember one time
you asked me who Marie Brizzard was? Well, you're
drinking her now."

And you know, it just kind of set everything up nicely for
me. As if maybe I'd come full circle. We had begun the end
of our marriage, Flick and myself, with him having Marie
Brizzard with another woman. And now it seemed as though
we were coming to the ending of the end of the marriage,
only I was the one having the Marie Brizzard this time.

I tell you, sometimes nothing makes much sense. So you
close your eyes and go to sleep when the not making sense
isn't rushing through you like a swarm of bees. Instead it is
just one bee trying to find enough food to make its way
home again.

28

When I woke up at Sam's, I was alone. He had left a chocolate doughnut on top of a note for me saying he had gone to work. I shouldn't have been there. I should have been with Evie. I shouldn't have been alone. I shouldn't have been without Flick. It was obvious I was confused. I may have understood that Flick didn't want me, I just didn't understand why. I may have understood that I had fallen in love with Sam, I just wasn't sure how I could have. And I didn't understand how I could have let Evie get into so much trouble. Was I always going to be so blind that I could not see my husband heading for adultery or my child heading for delinquency? Would there ever be a time in my life where things just came to me clearly?

I realize that reading your own child's diary is horrible, but when I had seen it on the floor under the bed the day before, wouldn't I have been even more horrible not to pick it up and see what she was going through? Maybe I could

help her. Maybe I could understand some things. Maybe I
could understand why she hated me so much. Why she
hated herself so much. So, I pulled Evie's diary out of my
pocketbook and read it on Sam's porch, eating my chocolate
doughnut.

She seemed to draw pictures more than anything. There
were strange drawings of black spiders swooping down on
black abstract blocks and black circles. There were faces,
drawn distorted and shaded in with a heavy pencil. There
were a few dark poems that went on about life, love, death
and politics. And I thought about how remarkable it was
that my sweet little Evie was so involved with politics at
thirteen when I was barely interested in it at thirty-four.

She had written only one journal entry. It started off
saying:

> My life has changed radically since I last wrote
> to you. I just haven't been able to deal with all the
> bad vibes. I nearly lost my mind.
> I still hate her. She won't get off my back. I hope
> I'm never like her.

It didn't take a genius to figure out who she was talking
about. But that didn't bother me as much as the black
drawings. Hating her mother was normal. The black drawings were morbid.

Then she went on to talk about most of the usual stuff you
write about when you're thirteen—boys, periods, girlfriends,
breasts—but the thing is, even that seemed so much deeper
than the things I wrote today. God, I mean there I was
writing down crap in my daily reminder with smiley faces,
saying things like, "Just a regular Morristown day, but on a
scale of 1–10, I'd give it a 10!!!! I love Morristown!!!!"

She was so honest.

I was so cheery and trite.

I stuck her diary back in my pocketbook and took a long walk and tried to think. Sam lived three miles from the Morristown Square but that's where I found myself. I loved going there and sitting on the benches next to the business-people eating their sack lunches. I loved remembering the time when I was the Little Miss Junior Tot Christmas Elf and Santa and I gave out toys under the same dark oaks and light sycamores where the businesspeople ate their lunches. I loved getting up and crossing the streets with the seeing-eye dogs and their trainers; walking down to the Morris County Savings Bank, standing in front of its brass trimmed doors, remembering the time when I first became an official teller and balanced right off the sheet: credits—zero, debts—zero, ten thousand dollars accounted for in my bank drawer. And if I had made a little mistake, someone would have thrown five cents in from the kitty and told me to try harder the next day. It was all so easy then.

I walked around some more and passed Macy's again, remembering how I spent my whole first paycheck there on snowboots and a mohair sweater and cap when it was still Bamberger's. Then I headed back to Sam's. It was a long walk uphill, but he still wasn't home. And I guess I must have exhausted the search for clues into my own life, because after snooping into Evie's privacy, I began to snoop into Sam's. And hell, I didn't even know what I was looking for. All I knew was that it was the first time I'd been alone in his house without him and if I didn't try to find out what I could about him, I would have been a fool. Or a man. No woman I knew would ever miss this kind of opportunity.

There were some pictures of him skiing with other women. That was good. They weren't too recent. That was good, too. There were some love letters. Pretty steamy. Pretty boring, but pretty steamy. But there weren't any naked photos in them and there weren't any girlie magazines either. Good, good and good. I liked a man who didn't look at girlie magazines. That kind of man seemed to be a breed apart from the average man who did. It was as if the women in their lives were sufficient enough for them. That's the way a woman likes to think her man thinks, too.

Sam had some pictures of his parents, but not an excessive amount of pictures of his mother.

He didn't line up the soup cans in alphabetical order and his socks weren't all tied up and matching. He hadn't started wearing thongs or bikini underwear the way Flick had. He wore white cotton boxers.

No love gels were under his bed. He had a lot of money. A lot of it. He had six or seven bank accounts.

He had real food in his refrigerator. Eggs. Tomatoes. Bacon. V-8 Juice. Leftover corned beef. And batteries. He kept batteries and film in the cheese section.

There wasn't much he needed, but a woman's touch would have been a good thing for Sam. He was the kind of man a woman wanted to touch, too.

I was just reading the last letter from an old girlfriend who called him "J. J." when he walked in and caught me. But all he said was, "Is that from Carol? She's a nice woman. She lives up in Vermont with her husband now. You two will have to meet each other someday."

I was horrified to have been caught, but he came over to where I sat. On a chair. Inside his closet. Next to all the boxes of old letters I'd pulled down. He held his hand out for me. I took it. He said, "You can look at that later. I need to tell you what happened about Evie."

"What? Is it bad, Sam?" Suddenly, I couldn't swallow. It sounded like an emergency. "They're not going to take her away from me are they?"

He shook his head and smiled. "No, Pammy. Whatever gave you that idea? You sound like such a kid."

"You looked so solemn, Sam. I thought something was wrong."

"Not at all. I was just watching you, I guess. Listen, I got up early and went to see a friend of mine about Evie's little VCR incident—he's a judge—and he said there wouldn't be any problem. He just wants her to write him a letter every week for a couple of months to let him know what she's up to. That's it. How you want to deal with her is another matter, but on this end, the legal end, it's all taken care of." He stood up and held his hand out to me. "Want to go get some breakfast?"

"Sam! How am I ever going to thank you?"

"Oh, you don't need to thank me," he said, pulling me up. "Just let me be your trim tab for a while."

"What's a trim tab?"

"You forgot what the trim tab is already?" he joked. Then he did the cutest thing. He held his arms out like he was a plane, bent his elbow down and pointed to the imaginary wing. "A trim tab," he said, leaning over to kiss me, "is what stabilizes the plane. God, you're beautiful this morning."

29

I wasn't sure how I was going to conduct my life from here on out. I wasn't sure how I was going to handle things. I mean, I'm not really sure you do know what you're going to do about something until it comes right up to you and says, "Here I am. Fix this." We think something is going to come up and slap us in the face and instead it ends up patting us on the back. We think something will be good for us and instead it turns out to be a kick in the head.

Sometimes I think if we could just turn our thinking completely around—not think about half the things we usually think about, and think about the other half for a change, the half we think isn't important—our lives would work out fine.

How do we get so wrong? How do we go from starting out thinking about food and love and a safe place to stay, to thinking about money and power and looking good? At what

179

point do we go from what's really important to who really
cares?

I'm thinking it cuts in early, at six or seven when we can't
get all the things we see on the commercials between
cartoons, but that it gets indelibly set in us at thirteen—at
thirteen, when we hate ourselves the most; when we think
everyone else hates us even more than we hate ourselves;
when we lie in our bed, crying, fantasizing about somebody
coming along with enough money to get us out of here, out
of our lives.

That's when we begin to think about the money. How
much would it take to get us out? We realize it would take a
lot of cash. There are so many things to consider. For
instance, you'd have to have more money than your aunt
Harriet, who has so much she can afford a bean-shaped pool
in her backyard. Why? Because if you left poor, you'd
know she'd be back home shaking her head feeling sorry for
you. And one of the reasons you'd be leaving in the first
place would be so nobody would think anything except
wonderful things about you.

And then you'd have to consider the clothing and the car.
If you go out in rags driving a Duster, then what sort of exit
would that be? Everyone would stand in the middle of the
street with their hands shielding their eyes from the sun and
watch you drive away and feel sorry that you're such a
vagabond.

And you'd have to consider your friends. You couldn't go
with your best friend, because chances are that at thirteen,
everyone likes your best friend more than you, because at
thirteen everyone likes everyone but you. And this isn't
your best friend's exit. It's yours. So your best friend can't
go with you. You're leaving your life to show people how
much they are going to miss you, not how much they're
going to miss your friend.

So. You have to leave with a star. You have to ride out of town on the arm of a celebrity so everyone will take notice. Which is maybe why celebrities are so important to us. Somehow things have gotten so screwed up in this world that we think the only time we're important is if we're getting a lot of attention. How does that even track?

I don't know. All I know is that when I was a little girl, when I was Tangerine, I used to think Elton John would see me standing by the fence at school and pick me up and carry me away. He'd see the prettiness behind the ugliness that everyone else saw. And I'd see the handsomeness behind his weird face—weird for a thirteen-year-old, which is why I had to pick him. I mean, I needed somebody who needed me, too. I tried the real good looking celebrities out, but I'd get to the point in my fantasy where they didn't need me and the dream would begin to fade away. But Elton John, he needed me. I could tell by listening to his music. And I needed him. And we spent a good amount of time running away together when I was thirteen. We spent so much time together, in fact, that now when I see him on television, I still think nobody understands him but me. And I don't even know the guy.

But that is not the point.

I don't know what the point is. If I did, maybe my little daughter wouldn't be so unhappy now. Maybe I could take her in my arms and tell her something that would get her through thirteen. But I tell you, a mother with the best intentions cannot even do that.

No. The best you can do for your daughter at that age is to keep your ear to the beat of that child and really hear what they have to say. And be quick to change with their changing.

But obviously I didn't know how to do that. I tried, but, Jesus, the minute she saw me, she was ready to fight. I said, "Evie, do you feel sorry for what you did?" All I needed was to feel a little remorse from her and then I'd tell her what Sam had worked out.

But she wasn't giving any away. "Sorry for what?"

"For stealing, you little thief. What do you think?"

"Oh," she said, taunting me. "I thought you meant was I sorry I was born. And the answer is, I'm sorry I was born to you."

Sometimes you just snap. You know what I mean? Sometimes everything builds up and builds up and builds up until your resistance is so low that you just can't take hearing one more damn time that you are a bad mother. Chances are you've been saying that very thing over and over to yourself and then, boom, your child drops the other shoe, the other lead boot, and that's it. You lose your cool. All right, so I'd left Flick. So I was seeing Sam. But all of Evie's friends were going through the same things with their parents and they weren't stealing VCRs and talking trashy to their mothers.

I was so angry I wanted to kick her. I began cramming her things in her suitcase. Banging drawers open and shut; pulling the drawers out and throwing them on the floor. She started to get scared. She began crying and yelling, "Mom, what are you doing?"

And then Miss New Jersey came sticking her nose in nobody's business. "What on earth is going on here?" she asked.

Evie cried, "Nana, make her stop. Mom, stop. What are you doing?"

"Mother," I said, through my clenched teeth, "you stay out of this. And I mean it." I grabbed the suitcase, I grabbed Evie and I literally dragged both of them out to the car. "I am going to take you back home to your father. I'm sick of you. I can't stand the sight of you another minute. I can't handle you. I can't stand you. I don't even want to see you again after this."

"Mom!" she cried from the backseat. "I'm sorry! I'm sorry!"

She tried to talk to me. I didn't know what I wanted to do, but listening wasn't it. I just wanted to drive straight up to Flick, drop her off, show him what a horrible thing she'd turned into, what a horrible thing I'd turned into, how it was all his fault.

The speed limit was fifty-five but I was going seventy, seventy-five, eighty. I was so angry I couldn't take my foot off the accelerator. It was just my luck that some New Jersey cop would pull me over. This, of course, did nothing to help my mood. I whipped out my license, shoved it at him and listened to Evie crying the tiniest little cry from the backseat while I watched the policeman strolling back to his patrol car.

In the tiniest most desperate little voice, to match her desperate little cry, Evie said, "I'm sorry, Mommy. Please take me back with you. Please don't leave me. I don't want to go."

It was the first time she had called me "Mommy" in a long, long time. I held on to the steering wheel tightly and tried not to cry myself. I felt awful. There wasn't any chance I was ever going to take my Evie back to Flick unless I went with her. I didn't know what was wrong with me. There were just too many things going on for me to focus on to get one of them under control.

The highway patrolman returned with my speeding ticket, which I had to sign, right under the date. That's when I noticed my mistake. My big mistake. It was the day after Evie's birthday. I had forgotten my little Evie's thirteenth birthday.

30

"It's okay, Mom," Evie said, as we drove back into town. "Don't take it so hard. Daddy forgot, too."

"Oh, baby!" I was crushed. I took her straight to Macy's and bought her everything on one of Flick's credit cards. I mean everything. Three bathing suits, her first pair of high heels, her first bra, a backpack, more black clothes. Somewhere around the black clothes the guilt began to wear off. "Evie, why all the black, sweetheart?"

"I don't know. I like it," she said, putting a black vest over a black long-sleeved T-shirt. Then I remembered what I was like at that age. I wore a black cape and necklaces with strange charms around my neck. And bell-bottoms. And elephant pants. I tried out everything trying to find my style. My mother wouldn't let me wear the clothes I wanted, so I used to wear the clothes she wanted me to wear, and when I left the house to go out with my girlfriends, I'd slip behind a bush and make a superman change into the real

Pammy. Did I really want to do that to my little girl? Did I really want to stifle her and keep her from trying things out?

No. That is not a good mother.

So, for one solid week, one more week of Flick not riding up on a white horse to take me back, I began to call her "Fern." And just when I got used to calling her "Fern," another week passed and she said, "Mom, don't call me that anymore. I'm going to be Evie again."

"Okay." I didn't know much, but I knew enough not to ask her why she'd changed her mind. She'd tell me eventually if she wanted.

But I did ask her why she stole the VCR. She'd said it was because she had wanted to have something to remember her daddy by. Her plan had been to go back home, get the home videos we had made at Christmas, and then she could always watch them if she missed him too much. "If Nana would just break down and buy something new for a change, I probably wouldn't have stolen it. But she doesn't ever have anything new. Anyway, that's why I wanted it."

We had just walked down to the mailbox to mail her second letter to the judge and now we were sitting on the porch, talking, waiting for Miss New Jersey to finish making dinner. The fireflies were out in droves. I could tell Evie wanted to talk about something, but it's funny about kids. You can't ask them because they won't tell you a damn thing. But if you just sit it out and wait for it, it'll all come pouring out. "Evie," I said, trying to open things up a little for her. "You won't have to miss your daddy for long. We just needed a little time apart. We'll work things out."

"You mean you just need to give him enough time to get rid of Audrey."

"Well, maybe that's what I mean. But he'll come around."

"Man, I *hate* her. She makes me feel like I'm six years old. She always sticks her moron self right up in my face and then says something to me in this creepy baby talk while she winks at Dad. And Dad just about falls all over himself every time she opens her mouth. Plus, she has ugly teeth and the creepiest breath.''

"She does?'' I, of course, was glad to hear all of this because I am this little girl's mother and a big part of me was always worried that Audrey had taken her over, as well. "But you were always talking to her,'' I said, baiting her for more.

"She was always talking to me. She wanted to know everything about me. Like if I had a boyfriend. Who my girlfriends were. Like I was going to tell her anything.'' Evie swatted at a mosquito.

"She's pretty, though, don't you think? It took me a long time to see how pretty she was. I mean, I used to think she was plain.'' God, I couldn't stop myself.

"She's a dog. I don't like her.''

She stopped talking and I could tell she wasn't going to give me any more on old Audrey, so I changed the subject and asked her about the boy/girl party she'd gone to the night before. Miss New Jersey had told her she couldn't go because the last time she had gone to a boy/girl party was when she broke loose with some loose girls and stole the VCR. But Evie had assured me it was a different crowd. And she wasn't so mad about things anymore. So I had trusted her and told her it was okay. Now she was back home, and she was sweet and innocent again, but my mother and I, of course, were not talking to each other because of this.

"Tell me about the party,'' I said. "Was it fun?''

God, her little face lit right up. "It was a swimming party. We didn't dance, we just swam. And guess what, Mom?''

"What?''

"The boys got out and cut the cake with their hands so the girls didn't want any so we just kept swimming." Then she got excited, and dammit, she looked just like Flick when she got excited. She dribbled the same imaginary basketballs. "Oh, but this one girl, Delia, she was so gross. She *ate* it. But nobody likes her."

"Why?"

"I don't know. She's noxious."

Great. What the hell did "noxious" mean? I sat there and pretended to understand.

Finally Evie said, "Mom, can I ask you something?"

"Sure, Evie. Anything."

"Okay. Well, do you have your heart set on this beauty pageant thing?"

"Don't you?"

"Not really."

"Why not?"

"I don't know. I'm not like those girls. I don't fit in with them or something. Like, do your remember that Young Miss Teen Georgia? The one with the red hair and those big boobs?"

I laughed. "Yep. She was heading straight for Atlantic City, wasn't she?"

"No kidding. Me and Macayla were standing next to her, you know, before the interviews? And Macayla said, 'Brenda, show Evie what's in your pocketbook.' So, she opened it, you know, and you know what was in there? It was this pin in the shape of a crown. And she said it was in there just in case they asked her what was in it. Can you imagine what I'd say if they asked me what was in my pocketbook? I think I probably had cigarettes and condoms in mine."

"Condoms!"

"I'm just joking, Mom. God, you never listen to anything I'm saying."

She sounded just like me trying to talk to Flick. "I'm sorry, Evie. Go on. I won't interrupt again."

"Well, all I'm trying to say, is that's my idea of what a beauty queen is supposed to be like. And I don't think I'm like that. I don't think I'm anything like Brenda. Brenda's all makeup and nerve endings. I'm just this little kid who worries all the time why all the girls at school have started their periods when I haven't started mine."

Suddenly I saw everything so clearly. I had been doing the same thing to Evie that Flick had been doing to books. He'd read a book and twist it and turn it into what he wanted it to say instead of what the author meant for it to say, the same way I'd been twisting and turning Evie into something that she had never wanted to become. I didn't want her to be Brenda either. I didn't want her to spend the rest of her life worrying if her hair was okay. I didn't want her spraying her little bottom with hairspray to keep her bathing suit from riding up for the rest of her life. I didn't want her presenting herself to the world the way I had presented myself to the world for the past thirty-four years.

Evie didn't need to spend her life doing that. She was already perfect as herself. Sure, she may have had thighs that were a little too big. She might not even be as pretty as me. But did that really matter? Maybe if I left her alone for a while, she'd have a better shot at being Evie than I'd ever have at being Pammy.

"Mom, Nana's got plans to take me to New York to get my hair dyed brown and to get me brown contacts."

"Are you kidding?"

"No. She thinks dark hair and dark eyes show up better on stage."

"Oh, my God!" I laughed. "Did I ever tell you that I always wanted blond hair?"

"Every day of my life, Mom."

"Well, if I had hair like yours, I'd never be unhappy again." I stroked her beautiful hair and listened to my mother banging pots around in her kitchen, putting the plates on the table, taking the pots off the stove. I thought about how sad she was going to be when I told her that Evie wasn't going to be in the pageant. I thought about how happy Evie was going to be.

"All right, Evie. You don't have to do the pageant. I'll get you out of it."

"Man, is that a load off my chest," she said, sounding like a little grownup.

"Evie," I said, taking her in my arms and hugging her. "You know, it's okay if you haven't started your period. A lot of girls don't start their periods until they're fourteen. And you know something else?"

I could tell she was embarrassed. She pressed her face under my arm and said, "What?"

"I know you worry about your breasts, too. But you don't need to. I didn't even get both of mine until well after I was sixteen. God, they didn't even match at first."

"I would have died, Mom."

"I did. Can you imagine. I stuffed everything in my bra. Socks, Kleenex, panties. And I wore a lot of big shirts."

I could feel her grinning on my chest. It made me feel so good. "Thanks, Mom," she said.

"You're welcome. Now tell me something? What the hell does 'noxious' mean?"

Evie laughed. "I'm not really sure. I think it means harmful or something. Did I use it wrong?"

"Well, Evie," I said, ruffling her hair, "I'd be the last to know."

Then Joe opened the door and said, "Your mother has dinner ready. You know, when I was in the army we weren't allowed to sit around. We had to keep busy. Keep moving. Eh? Eh?''

"Okay, Joe. We're up. We're up," I said, pulling Evie off the porch steps.

"You're going to eat your dinner tonight, little girl," he said, pointing at Evie. "It'll put some hair on that chest of yours."

"Grandaddy Joe, believe me. It's not hair I want on my chest." She went over to him and wrapped her arms around him and for one brief, shining moment I thought I saw that old man smile.

31

There are times when I feel really screwed up, but I feel most screwed up when I'm with my mother. That's when I'm the most deranged and incompetent. For instance, when I entered her kitchen to tell her that Evie wasn't going to be in the pageant, I couldn't do it. One stupid little sentence and I couldn't get it out of my mouth.

So she said, "You got a letter from Flick."

And I don't know. Something about the way she said it really pissed me off. "Where is it?" I asked, watching her wipe her hands on a dish towel, which made me even more mad because she does not believe in paper towels and that really pissed me off, too, for no good reason. She always says there isn't one thing a paper towel can do that a good dish towel can't do better.

She pulled the letter out of her apron and handed it to me. Then she left so I could read it. That was unusual since she had been breathing down my business for as long as I could remember. But I was glad she left because frankly, and I don't know why, but sometimes all my mother has to do is breathe and it drives me up the wall.

Here is what my husband had to say to me after all the long confusing weeks without him. He said:

Dear Pammy,

I write to tell you how happy your letter made me. You said so much in your letter. I'm not even sure you realize how much you said. First, you are right. There is always something missing between us. But, if there weren't, we'd not be us, we would be each other.

You also said, and I quote, "I've just noticed for the first time what you always were." This may be complicated, but try and follow the line of reason. Okay. Since who I was, is who I am now, and who I am is who I will become, and who I become is always, always, who I was, and you loved who I was, then I know you know now that you will always love me.

Your phone call startled me. But then I received your letter and was able to piece together all the madness. What you've been trying to say is not that you were going to leave me, as I first thought, but that you wanted me to pull us back together. You wanted me to see that the gap between us, the gap that I tried filling with Audrey, was a gap that should be left open with nobody filling it. I'm beginning to understand this now.

I want you to understand that what you said when you called me may have been that you wanted a divorce, but what you meant was that we really belonged together. I was glad when I finally figured out that's what you meant to say.

   If this letter beats me up there, please hold on tight. I'll be following right behind. First, I have to undo some of the damage that I've done.

Love, Flick

I mean, what kind of crap was that? What was he saying? He was obviously drowning in Deconstructionism, the poor fool. Well, it didn't matter. What mattered was that he had finally figured out what I'd been trying to tell him these last few long months. That it didn't take a college genius to figure out what someone was trying to say. All you had to do was listen to the tone in the person's voice. But with Flick, nothing was ever that simple. Everything had to be analyzed and mulled over until he'd driven himself and everyone else insane.

It was funny. I finally had a chance to take Flick back and I was wondering if I could take the pushing and pulling that came with all that thinking he did. I may have worried constantly over little things, but he constantly worried over things that didn't even exist.

Miss New Jersey came back in and sat down next to me. "So, what did the college boy say?"

"Nothing much." I could feel my jaw tighten. Suddenly I was about to explode. That was the way it was with my mother and me. Things could be going fine and then for no apparent reason I'd want to jump out of my skin. "He said his studying was coming along. He sends his love."

"Come on, Pamela. What did he really say? Flick has never sent his love to me."

I got up to wash the dishes. I knew exactly what I was letting myself in for. The sink was my mother's terrain. She would let me dry, if I dried them right, but she didn't like

me to wash. But this time she must have seen that I was
going to do them, regardless. I started washing them in the
double sinks and right away I could feel her behind me
getting ready to leap in if I didn't do everything exactly
right.

This is her routine. She turns on the water. She wets a
plate. She turns the water back off. Then she does another
plate. Every time she has ever turned the water off, for as
long as I can remember, I would feel like throwing something at the back of her head.

But this time I was going to do them my way, with the
sink full of water and thick suds and I could plunge my
hands in. None of that off again, on again mess.

I knew I was testing her but I couldn't stop myself.

I filled one side of the double sink with soap and water
and began washing. As I did I could hear her sighing behind
me. Then I began to fill the other sink with rinse water.
Right away here comes her hand and she cuts it off. I waited
until I had another dish ready for rinsing and I turned it back
on. This time I turned the water down, not off, mind you,
but just about halfway. She sighed again and here comes the
hand again and off it went. I tried counting to ten, then to
twenty to keep from exploding as I washed a third dish in
the soapy water. I had it ready and I cut the water back on
and rinsed it. Then something perverse rolled over in me
and I turned the water down until only the thinnest possible
trickle was coming out. I waited for the sigh and watched
for the hand, hoping it would come. And it did. As the
water was cut off I picked up a perfectly dry plate and
smashed it into a hundred pieces on the faucet. "Jesus
Christ! No wonder I'm so damned screwed up!"

I turned around to wring her neck but she wasn't ac-
knowledging my little explosion—the same way she had
never acknowledged all the little explosions I had ever had

around her before. Instead, she quietly picked the broken pieces out of the sink and then she began to dry the others.

Well, here is Miss New Jersey's fucked-up drying technique. A dish has to drip dry for at least three full minutes before you can pick it up and buff it dry with a dish towel. Three minutes per plate, which meant ten dishes had always taken at least thirty minutes. Then there were the cups, the saucers, the silver.

I'd read in some magazine once that men kill women in the bedroom and women kill men in the kitchen. Well here we were in the kitchen and my mother was killing me. Hell, maybe she had killed me years ago and I'd just been walking around dead and didn't know it.

This time as I watched her, I noticed her reflection in the mirror on the sideboard and found myself doing something really weird. I began copying her every move, her every gesture: what she did with her mouth, her eyes, how she stood with her feet together but her toes pointing out, how she pushed her hair back with her left hand when it went to the right and her right hand when it went to the left. I copied how she tipped her tongue on the right edge of her mouth, followed by her pursing her lips when she concentrated, how she held her hands up with her wrists flexed and away from her to dry. It was sort of like going down the checklist before you took off in a plane, but the difference was, in a plane you were taught how to climb out of a stall. As far as I knew, nobody had ever been able to teach a woman how to climb out of her mother's mold.

Did I really do all those things, I had to ask myself. And the answer was, I found them too easy to do. When I did them, I didn't feel as if I were copying my mother, I felt as if I'd been doing them all along. I may have broken free of her little habits, like the way she washed her dishes, but I couldn't escape the way our hands looked so much alike when we held things, or the way our mouths set in exactly the same way when we were upset by our daughters.

"Dammit!" I said, exploding again. I desperately needed to see her change the expression on her face—to have an expression for once, besides total control. "Why does every stupid dish take three minutes! Don't you realize how much time you waste?"

Nothing again.

"Mother! It's time we talked," I said, practically screaming at the top of my lungs.

And, of course, she simply turned away and began to walk out of the room. But I grabbed her first. "Don't you walk out on me. I've got a thing or two to tell you."

She looked at me horrified. I'd never screamed at her before like this. Her mouth was open and I moved in for the kill, completely out of control. "Damn you, this is all your fault! Everything is your fault. You have everything so damned organized and perfect that's there no way to even breathe around here. No wonder I married Flick. Hell, I would have married Joe Schmoe to get out of this stupid house. Do you understand that?"

She reached for the sink and held on to it. "You don't have to yell at me."

"Yell at you? I don't have to yell at you? Fine. But why don't you try yelling at me for once? I've heard you yell at Joe. You don't have any problem yelling at him. You've yelled at him so many times, I wasn't about to yell at Flick. And maybe that's what I needed to do. But no. You taught me how to be the perfect little lady and I've perfected myself right out of my marriage. Did you know that, Mother? Hmmm? That I've left Flick. And now I see that you're as much to blame for this as I am. Jesus! Was I blind or what? What have you done to me?"

Still, my mother just stood there. I was furious. I stormed

over to her and turned the water on. "I want the water on! Do you hear me? On, with a capital O! And you can forget the Legacy of Beauties. I'm not going through with it and neither is my daughter. As a matter of fact, she's not ever going to enter another damn beauty pageant for the rest of her life. Now I know you can't understand this but that's the way it's going to be."

She started to turn the water off but I reached over and stopped her. "No, you listen for a change, because I'm not going to repeat it or argue about it or ask your approval or anything. You want to know why Flick never sent his love, Mother? Huh? Do you? Speak up, Miss New Jersey. This is an interview question. Why oh why does your son-in-law never come to visit?"

My mother stood, quietly, with her hands on the edge of the sink. She was beginning to look so worn out. She seemed so far away, as though I'd slugged her in her perfectly flat fifty-year-old stomach and knocked the wind out of her. I wanted to take her in my arms and say, "Oh, Mother. Don't you understand that at some point it becomes ridiculous trying to keep such a flat tummy? Don't you understand that most people aren't like this? Don't you ever just want to break down and enjoy food for a change?" But I couldn't say that. For one thing, she was my mother and I was her daughter and I was still washing dishes the way she wanted me to wash them after all these years. Even as angry as I was, I still reached over and turned the water back off. Why? Because the guilt was beginning to set in on me. Guilt, though, made me even more angry. "Well, Miss New Jersey, the reason your son-in-law doesn't come for visits is because you are too much of a snob. You can't stand him and he knows it. You've never even made the effort."

I could tell I was pushing her to the limit. Through clenched teeth she said, "No, Pammy. That isn't true."

So I screamed, "Well, what the hell is true then, Mother?"

She whipped her head around and stared right in my face and now she was the one yelling. "You really want me to tell you about Flick?"

"Puh-lease!"

"Okay, I'll tell you about Flick. Have you ever had a girlfriend who began to date someone you didn't like and you thought, 'Christ, what can I say to her?' And you think, nothing. I can't say a damn thing. Well, that's the way it was with Flick."

"So," I said, snidely. "You finally admit it, Mom. You hate Flick."

She shook her head. "No, Pammy. I don't hate Flick. It's just that he's about the most obsequious person I've ever met."

Oh, great. Finally she revealed the great mystery of her feelings for Flick and I didn't even know what the hell "obsequious" meant. And I couldn't ask her, because, well, I just couldn't.

"Well, for your information, Mother, Flick and I are thinking about getting a divorce."

She threw her head back and began laughing. "God, I thought you'd never tell me. Pammy, you don't know how relieved I am."

"God, Mother! I can't believe how uncaring you are. I didn't say we *were* getting a divorce. I said we were talking about it. And you're happy about it."

"That's not what I meant," she said, grabbing my arm and pulling me back to the table. "I've been trying for weeks to tell you about me and Joe, but I knew when you weren't telling me about you and Flick, that I couldn't tell you my news. I thought you'd hate me for getting divorced."

"Are you kidding me? You and Joe are divorcing, too?" and just like that, I wasn't mad anymore.

It was my mother who was mad. "We have divorced. I've had the poor thing coming around for weeks now just so you'd think we were together. You're such a spoiled brat. Nobody's allowed to have any feelings but you. Nobody can go through trauma, just little Tangerine, my big pain in the ass. It's a miracle I didn't go crazy raising you."

She got up and turned the water on and left it running. "Is this what you want, Pammy? Because whatever my little Pammy wants, my little Pammy gets. I'm telling you, Joe is going to be so relieved he doesn't have to play this game any longer. He always said to me, 'Lillian, you are ruining that child's life spoiling her the way you do.' And he was right. Look at you. You've got a mother who loves you. A daughter who's crazy about you, and you're miserable."

"Mother!"

"No. You listen to me now. You want to know what miserable is? I'll tell you what miserable is. You know how I never told you about your father? How when you brought him up, I walked off?"

My heart stopped. I didn't want to say anything. I'd dreamt of this moment all my life. I'd fought for this moment ever since I had found out what a father was. I had pictured him, had conversations with him, turned him into a tall man with brown hair and laughing green eyes and a wry smile. I'd turned him into a man who missed me and thought about me with every breath he took.

Suddenly my mother was crying. "Oh God, Pammy, I can't tell you this."

She put her hands up to her face but I grabbed them and pulled them away. "No, Mom, you've got to tell me."

"Don't hate me. Please don't hate your old mother. I was so young. I was what, seventeen. And there were so many men around me just like you had all those men around you.

Remember how I wouldn't let you date anyone unless I knew everything about them? And remember all those curfews I had you on?''

"Yes, Mother. Keep going."

"Oh, God. How do I say this? I think it was this guy from Jersey City. You look a little like him, the same hair, the same green eyes. But I was never sure."

"You mean, you don't know who my father is?" I asked, pulling her back down to sit with me.

"That's right. I don't know, Pamela. I just don't know."

We sat there not talking for a long time. Then she said, "You know, you just didn't do that kind of thing back then, go with different men like that. Well, you did it, but you didn't talk about it. You never talked about it like you do today. I'm not even sure you did it as much as you do it today. I didn't do it much. But I obviously did it enough to get into trouble."

She began to cry, softly. But she didn't take her hands to her face this time to wipe her tears away. She just let them come. "I didn't know what to do. Abortion wasn't an option. My mother could never have handled it. Never. She was like you. You remind me so much of her, bless her heart. So delicate and fragile. Everything was so breakable. So, then Joe came along." She straightened her back and talked even softer. "He wasn't somebody I *love* loved, you understand. But he was somebody who loved me. He knew I was pregnant with you and he loved me anyway."

She reached over and put her hand on the back of my neck and smiled. "I know you never liked him, but he was good for me. He got me out of my mother's house. He married me."

She took my hand up to her mouth and began kissing it. Her tears felt so different on my skin than somebody else's tears. I couldn't explain if I tried. They just felt, well, sadder. "Oh, the day you were born was the most wonderful day in my life. I never regretted being pregnant with you. You were such a joy. You still are."

I thought about how happy my mother had been when I had been crowned Miss South Carolina. She just about drove Flick crazy, because she went with me everywhere. My early years were the best years of her life.

"I'm sorry if I messed you up, Pammy. I know what I'm telling you hurts."

"No, Mom," I laughed. "It's just going to be a little weird getting used to the fact that I don't know who my father is, even though I never did know who he was."

"How about Flick? Are you going to be okay with that, Pammy?"

"Well, I don't know. I've sort of been seeing Sam. Or didn't you figure that out yet?"

"Ahhh! She's takes me for a fool," she said to the ceiling. Then to me she said, "You know, you've got to go with the one you feel the most comfortable with. That's the ticket. That's why I went with Joe. You don't see what I see with Joe. With you, he presents himself the way he thinks you need to see him. He really isn't like that, Pammy. He's a sweet man. And he's my best friend. I can talk to him about anything. I always could. That's why I married him. Then you were born and he lived with us for the first year or so. But then I asked him to leave because, well, because I didn't love him. And then later, I asked him back because, well, who the hell knows why we do anything? I think I asked him back because I didn't think anyone else could love me as much as he did."

"So, why did you get divorced?"

"Who the hell knows? Maybe I just don't like being married. Does it really matter? Joe and I will still play golf.

He'll still come by for dinner. He'll still be hanging around long after you've decided what the hell you're going to do with your harem of men.''

I got up from where I was sitting and went to hold her. ''I love you, Mom.''

''Yeah. That's nice about a mother and daughter. They may hate each other all the time, but they know they love each other, too. You can't always say that about a man.'' She got up and walked to the sink. She stuck a dish under the running water. Then she turned the water off and soaped the dish. Then she turned the water back on, rinsed the dish, turned the water back off. And you know what? It still drove me crazy.

''Pammy,'' she said. ''You've been a good daughter. You're a good girl. Sometimes I don't think I've told you that enough. But I have a feeling that you're going to know instinctively what road is good for you and your little girl.''

''I don't think I'm so good, Mom.''

She reached over and took my face with her soapy hands. ''Darling, just let me say this, okay. Staying married can be a good thing. Leaving a marriage can be a good thing. Not deciding anything right away can be a very good thing, too. It's like I'm telling you. If you're a good girl, whatever you decide to do, it's going to be the right thing for you. And you're a good, good girl, Pamela. You know how I know?''

''How?'' I sobbed.

''Because a mother just knows.''

32

God, I'm turning into my mother. Even down to the summer gloves I wear. And it's not so bad. Because I'm turning into my daughter, too.

Here we are, my mother, my wonderful mother, combined with my wonderful little daughter, all wrapped up into me. Just like my mother was to her mother and daughter. And her mother was to her mother and daughter. And undoubtedly her mother would have been to her mother and daughter. But I don't think they ever even thought that way back then. Just like I don't think my mother ever had to think as much as I have to think now. And I don't think I'll ever, ever have to think as much as my daughter will.

Poor old unsuspecting thing. There she is, happily being herself, with millions of troubles and changes just waiting around the corner to pounce on her. And me, with nothing to do but be amazed at the things she will have to face that I never had to even think about facing.

How green I was when I used to think some little girl would be so lucky to be my daughter. That I'd be able to do the mommy thing better than my mother did. And now my little girl comes along after all these years just to show me how wonderful my mother really is.

I am the lucky one. Because I have a good mother. And I have a good daughter. I even think my little girl is beginning to like me again.

It's funny, but when our children are growing up, they have to like us. It doesn't occur to us to think they won't. But then one morning we wake up and see that they are old enough to decide for themselves who they should like and not like, and we have to hold our breath and hope we pass the test. And we will be tested. I just hope that when I finally give my little girl the pair of summer gloves my mother gave me, she will love and respect me as much as I love and respect my mother now.

Summer gloves. I'm not sure why I wear them now. They still feel weird. I'm not sure why I do anything I do. If I did, maybe I would understand why I am about to take off in this little Cessna plane all by my myself.

I used to know why I did things. That's because I used to be Flick's wife and I did things for Flick. And who knows. Maybe when this is all over I'll still be his wife. But that wouldn't be the point.

The point would be that if I were ever his wife again, I'd be Pammy first. I would never go back to being crinoline straight up and down all day long.

See. That's the whole point. My daughter has taught me that much. She has taught me the importance of trying different things out even if sometimes that means doing some things backwards along the way. I mean, look how I am finally growing into my own person after I've already grown up and had a child. That's backwards, but it's working.

It's quite a lot like flying, where you steer with your feet and control speed with your hands. Sure, I feel strange flying. It's not something I intended to do. Frankly, I did not even know I was going to solo until I got in the plane with cranky old Vincent Cullingsworth, taxied down the runway and then he hopped out on me and said, "Give it a go."

Give it a go? Left to my own devices, I would never have given it a go. I would never have even left Flick. I would have stayed right where I was. Happy. Not even knowing how much happier I could have been if I hadn't been standing so still.

That was the bad part. Loving Flick so much, but not enough to notice how sad he was that I was standing still while he was going forward and moving ahead and leaving me behind. He must have been so frustrated. So confused. So lonely.

Well, I'm moving ahead now. It might not be in the same direction, but at least I am moving.

I take a deep breath and give it a go, taxiing down the runway, finally reaching sixty miles an hour and taking off. One thing about flying—once you have left that ground, you have committed yourself to something whether you like it or not.

Maybe that is how Flick felt when he committed adultery. I'm not excusing him. I'm just trying to understand him. Maybe he didn't know what he was doing, but once he'd done it, there wasn't any turning back.

I'm going up and up and up. It is a strange sensation. I can feel nothing under me. I cannot believe how calm I am. I cannot believe how scared I am. I cannot believe I have done this and it is all up to me to get me back down.

How in God's name will I ever get back down? I feel like flying around in circles forever, rather than trying a landing on my own.

Why have I done this to myself? I ask. All this time I was

taking flying lessons and I wasn't paying that much attention. I'd never remember to put my flaps down.

Why hadn't I just jumped out of the plane and run after Vincent Cullingsworth, kicking and screaming, "What in the hell do you think you are doing, leaving me alone like that? Are you insane?!"

And why had I never said that to Flick?

Well, you know what I think? I think it's like with Evie. We don't ask what we don't want to know. I remember the first time I found her Barbie doll taped naked to Ken so long ago. And I don't know. Maybe I put it back the wrong way and she noticed that I'd been there. Because it wasn't long after that when she came up to me and said, "Mommy, do you know what Macayla does?"

I had said, "What, honey?"

She had looked around to make sure her daddy wasn't listening, and she said, "She makes her dolls do bad things."

She may not have known what she was saying, but I am that little girl's mother and I could tell right away that she wasn't talking about Macayla. She was talking about herself, looking for my reaction to what she considered her evilness.

So, what did I do? I did what any mother who loves her daughter would do. I took her in my arms and I said, "Oh, honey. It's okay if Macayla does her dolls that way. I used to do the same things to my dolls. All girls do their dolls that way. It's normal." I remember her wiggling out of my arms, so relieved, to go off and play again.

I remember a lot of things now as I approach five hundred feet and bank to the left. For instance, I remembered to bank to the left! I also remembered to put my brakes on to stop the wheels from turning. Maybe a little too late, but at least I remembered. But that didn't mean I was going to remember to put my flaps down for landing.

Everything is so smooth in my New Jersey sky. And New

Jersey is so beautiful below. I am seeing the part of my state that other people who, when they think of Jersey, think of gas refineries and industrial trash, don't ever see. They don't see the farmlands and the mountains and the pastures and the waterfalls and Jockey Hollow Park where George Washington kept his men during the Revolutionary War. Just like when they go south, they don't see all the beauty there. They see poverty and ignorance and almost none of the nice things.

Well, I am trying to see things for what they really are now. And I am trying hard. It occurs to me that I cannot make this flight without God. I do not know enough about science and the lifts and drags that keep a plane up in the air. But I do know that there is something mysterious that makes a mother and a daughter finally bond together and I have to assume that it is this same mystery, this same divine intervention, that keeps me from dropping out of the sky.

The nose is pointing above the horizon. I am at two thousand feet and still climbing when I make my second turn. Following Vincent's instructions I level off at three thousand feet, cut back on the power and ease the air speed to 140, with the Garden State Parkway on my right and the blue green hills of Mendham on my left.

In the distance I can see the runways meeting in their triangle shape. Flying parallel to the field with only two more turns and a landing in front of me, something goes wrong. Suddenly the cockpit is filling up with smoke. I cannot breathe. My throat is constricted. I can't see the wingtips. I can't see the propeller. I can't see the windshield. But I can see the gauges. Frantically I check every gauge two times, three times, four times. They seem normal enough. But what would I know about normal? What would I know about gauges? Nothing is in the red zone. All I know is that I can smell burning oil and I am in this plane alone. I am going to drop out of this sky. I am going to die.

I say, "Oh, God! Oh, God! Get me through this. Hold my hand and tell me what the hell to do! I'm sorry I said 'hell.' I'm sorry for everything I've ever said and done. I am sorry for all of the messes I have made, and all of the messes other people have made that I have not forgiven them for."

I go on like this for some time. I can feel my beauty queen hand sweating through my mother's summer glove. The smoke begins to clear and, straining forward to see better, I make the next turn. I can see the sky ahead of me now, but I cannot see the ground for the smoke.

I now know I am going to crash and immediately I take stock of who is important to me. I know that Flick is at my mother's with my little girl. My precious little girl. I know that my mother is at the beauty parlor with her friends having her 1950s hair done. And I know that Sam is down below, watching me up above, waiting for me to come in so he can cut the back of my shirt off—a ritual they do when you first solo.

Finally, I am banking left again. And the plane starts to clear up. And the noise I was hearing turns out to be the noise of my imagination. New Jersey looks friendly below. I am thinking I am going to make it now. I may not have paid enough attention to my flying lessons, but I have probably paid enough attention to wing it. The same way I probably paid enough attention to the way my mother raised me, so I could wing it when it came time for me to raise my daughter.

As I turn onto the approach leg the smoke clears completely. The sky is radiant and the runway is directly in front of me. I am going to make it! And when I land, I'm going to have to make some pretty big decisions about the men in my life.

For instance, am I going to leave Flick alone, trapped in that deconstruction forever; or am I going to take him back and show him how to just plain straight construct? Or will I fly around with Sam and see where that takes me? Or will I, perhaps, try things alone for a change?

It's a lot to think about but first I just want to get this damned plane down.

As I ease back on the power, I remember to put my flaps down. I cannot believe I've remembered this. You have no idea how hard it is to remember something as easy as putting your damn flaps down.

I cut my power in order to glide down to the runway. I am actually going to make it! I know a lot more than I thought I ever knew. I know how to fly!

And as I give the plane just a little more juice to get it over the electric wires, I see what the problem was. I had flown over a pile of burning tires and a thick plume of smoke had found its way into my cockpit.

Only in New Jersey.

Isn't that something! Isn't that just like my damn crazy life? Isn't that just like everybody's life? First we see smoke. Then we get lost. Then we work our way through it with whatever we believe in that holds us together. Then we find our way home.

Just as I touch down I get this great idea and I push the throttle forward and increase the power. While Vincent and Sam are waving at me to slow down, I keep increasing it. I increase it some more and take back off. I know what I want to do now. I want to get off the ground. I want to get back up in the air. I want to think about everything just a little bit longer.

ABOUT THE AUTHOR

Sarah Gilbert has soloed and is working toward her pilot's license.